TRAPPED BY CLAWS

OF SEAS AND TIDES

JESSICA M. BUTLER

CONTENTS

Dedicated to all you out there who try so hard to be faithful, steadfast, practical, and pragmatic but know deep down you're a hot mess express who wants to be seen, valued, and loved.

Thank you for your faithfulness and steadfastness even when it hurts and no one sees.

You do matter. May you be seen, valued, and loved. And may someone wrap you tight in snuggly hugs and remind you of this soon.

OTTER IN THE WATER

A dark, serpentine shape shot out from beneath the stern of the ship, closing in on the lone otter.

I gasped, leaning out over the carved octopus figure at the back of the ship, my long auburn hair swinging over my shoulders. "Swim faster, little guy!" My fingers pressed hard against the painted wood.

What was that otter doing out here all alone? Where was its family?

The otter sliced through the deep-blue waters, but it stood no chance of escaping the enormous eel that chased after it. Even if it managed to get onto one of the small white stone islands that dotted the watery landscape, the eel could easily snatch the poor creature in its jaws.

I balled my hands into fists and struck the wood as I stared after the terrified creature. Its dark-brown tail swept desperately through the waters.

The poor baby!

It was all alone out here. And that giant green-and-yellow eel was bearing down on it, its long dorsal fin and sleek back slicing through the water.

The eel was going to eat it.

No!

Nature might be cruel, but that didn't mean I had to stay up here and watch the carnage.

I swept my hand down to the ring clip at my side, pulling up the mini-crossbow. It clattered against my wooden stew spoon and flint stick. Fingers steady, I loaded a blue bolt into the narrow slot. A single bolt was enough to stun most predators of the sea. Captain Hosvir might not approve of this, as it wasn't one of their enormous hunting otters at risk, but who cared? Let him be mad.

The wind was all but gone today. It had been that way for days. All I had to account for was the gentle rise and fall of the ship. I hooked my leg around one of the wooden tentacles, leaned down, aimed, and squeezed the trigger.

The blue bolt shot through the air, faster than the eel, almost as quick as the wave sliding over its lengthy body. With a sharp *thwick*, the bolt embedded in the eel's hide. The eel lurched back, its tail drooping down into the water. Its head spun about, bright-green eyes blinking as if in shock. Then it sunk out of sight.

Yes!

Success!

Half a breath more and I'd once again secured the mini-crossbow to my belt alongside the wooden spoon. Then I hopped back from the carved cephalopod onto the deck. I grabbed a sling, seized one of the knotted ropes, secured the sling, and cast the rope over the side.

The otter circled in the waters below, whimpering. As it rolled onto its back, I glimpsed its right paw. It was lighter and smaller, almost twisted or deformed.

Poor thing.

Was that why it was circling instead of swimming away? Maybe it had nowhere else to go. I certainly understood that.

2

Obviously, I had to help it. Otherwise, it'd be easy prey for whatever other predators lurked in these waters.

"Hang on, little guy!" I grabbed up the knotted rope, checked to ensure it was properly secured, and swung off the side of the ship.

My stomach dropped as I fell off the edge.

This was a move I'd struggled to learn when I first got on the ship. But weeks of practice allowed me to swing off the side of the ship and land on the stone. The otter had come alongside the table-sized island of smooth white rock and was now near the single trunk-like column in the island's corner.

Had to be quick. Didn't want to get clawed or bit.

Stooping down, I scooped the otter up. It was heavier and larger than it looked, about the size of a small child. Rivulets of water streamed off it, soaking my dress as I held it close.

But the otter didn't struggle or fight. It didn't even appear slightly frightened. It patted my cheek and pushed its whiskered snout against my face.

It smelled of fish, salt, wet fur, and algae, not quite as pleasant up close as from a distance.

Then it hugged me.

My heart melted. "Oh. Oh, little baby." What could I do but hug it right back?

That fishy, furry scent was no longer so jarring.

A knot of emotion formed in my throat. The first time anyone had hugged me in weeks, and it was an otter? Yeah. Actually…this wasn't so bad. Little baby was good at hugging.

"Come on. I'll get you to the ship, and then we'll get you some nice fish. Would you like that, baby?" I stroked its back, my posture relaxing.

The otter perked up, lifting its head from my shoulder. Whiskers twitching, it let out a series of sharp, trilling chirps.

I turned.

A dark shape shot toward us in the water.

Salt's bane!

Was that the same eel?

I'd hit it right in the body with that dart. The eel should have been out of it for another five or ten minutes. Similar bolts had taken down beasts far bigger than it.

But that yellow-and-green striping was so distinctive. It was the same one.

Adjusting my grip on the otter, I fished out another capped bolt from my pocket and seized the mini-crossbow at my side.

Why hadn't I just climbed back on the ship? This was what I got for delaying. At least I'd practiced this enough times to load it one-handed—

The otter wriggled and tore the crossbow out of my hand.

"Wait! What?" I struggled to hold onto the otter when it knocked the bolt from between my fingers too.

With a yelp, I fell back. The bolt rolled into the water, and the crossbow clattered onto the coarse white stone.

The otter leaped from my arms, snatched up the crossbow, and dove into the water.

The little bastard!

My hand went to my hip once more. Salt's bane! I wasn't wearing a dagger, and I'd left my paring knife in the kitchen. All I had was my stew spoon.

I sprang to the corner column of rock. Not even a pebble marred this island's surface, so there was nothing to throw. I cringed against the stone as the eel rose up out of the water.

"Mmmphhhhh—" The eel reared up out of the waves, water spilling from its squared head. It brought its jaws toward me.

Glaring, I pressed against the stone spire and struck the eel on the snout with the wooden spoon. "No! Go away!"

The eel pulled back, blinking. Its bright-green eyes practically glowed in the autumn sunlight. "You can't truly think that's going to work," it rumbled, its voice vibrating through the air.

My mouth fell open. Somehow an otter stealing my crossbow wasn't the strangest thing that was going to happen today.

OF EELS AND GRAVITY

he enormous eel tilted his head, his slanted, squared jaw opening. Instead of attacking, a laugh rippled out of him as he winked at me. "Didn't think that one through, did you, darling?"

I glared at him. Shifter fae, most likely. There were a few of them out this way, but why in all that was holy had he been chasing that otter?

Regardless, I didn't appreciate his tone. I stepped out from behind the spire and glared up at him, hands set on my waist with the wooden spoon still in hand. "I thought it through as much as anyone could. And at least I did something. Something is better than nothing."

Another laugh rolled from his jaws as he slid down in the water. He was now approximately at my eye level, his eyes dancing with mischief. He twisted a little more. The sunlight glistened on his sleek scales. "I don't know. That bit of wood is less than a toothpick." He looked me up and down. Even though he was an eel, it seemed he might be smirking. "But I like your spirit. You've got a lot of gumption for such a little human. Especially one with such dark, beautiful eyes."

"My eye color has precisely nothing to do with my ability to defend myself."

"True, but it does give me reason to comment on your beauty." He ducked his head down, the muscles through his body tightening. They pulsed and shuddered as he clenched his eyelids shut. His body collapsed downward, becoming a male mer whose lower half was an eel tail.

I sucked in a breath.

Oh. Wow.

How could he possibly claim I was attractive when he looked like that?

He maintained the same bold yellow and green striping, and—he was stunning. Somehow, even with such vivid colors, he was ethereally beautiful. Sharp cheekbones, defined lips, slanted but strong jaw, smooth brow, loose black curls, and bright-green eyes. So striking he made me ache. And yet there was something unsettling in his beauty.

Maybe it was his coloration. It certainly made his features and muscles appear all the more angular. And there was a sharp hunger in his eyes that had intensified now that he was no longer in the eel form. He sank into the water up to his waist, bobbing up and down into the waves as he studied me with that flirtatious smirk. He wore nothing but a claw bracelet that hugged his wrist so tight the claws pressed into his skin. "You really are remarkable," he said, as if entirely unaware of my reaction to him.

I snapped my mouth shut. What was I thinking? He was a fae. A shifter fae at that. And that meant he was dangerous. Of course he was gorgeous. Fae usually were. And shifter fae could adapt their appearances. If he hadn't had that bold striping and the strange color pattern, he'd have been impossible to resist. Even now, every inch of him radiated sensual beauty and grace.

"Enough with the flattery." I turned my face away.

He chuckled. His voice was smoother in this form. He folded his arms behind his head as he leaned back in the water. "There's never enough flattery when it comes to someone like you."

"I'm not fond of lies."

"I don't lie." He rolled forward and rested his folded arms on the stone. He cut his eyes up at me, smiling. The smile had an edge to it—like a predator sizing up its prey. "It certainly isn't a lie to say that you are very pleasant to look upon."

I stepped back, heart racing a little faster, my feet silent on the warm rock. A strange sensation buzzed through me, settling in my lower belly. "You *are* flattering me."

The waves lapped against him as he continued to smile and rake his gaze up and down my body. The sharpness in his eyes intensified.

A shiver tensed through me, almost too much for me to hide.

Damn him.

Those loose black curls of his begged me to run my fingers through them.

No, stop!

He murmured with amusement. "Flattery can be true. And in this case, it is. You're the prettiest creature I've seen in these parts."

A blushing heat crept up my throat and over my face. It wasn't hard to think of something to shut down this conversation. But I liked that he saw me. I liked the compliments too. Even if I shouldn't.

I shook my head. "Enough of that," I said, a little sharper than I intended.

It didn't affect him. "Ah, you're the practical sort. I embarrass you if I make too much of a fuss over you." He winked. As he looked me up and down again, he tapped his fingers on the stone. No—his claws. His fingernails were actually long, dark claws. "It would be so very hard for me to not make a fuss over you. Especially if you came back with me. Why don't you come to my home?"

Something flashed in his eyes as he asked this—a look almost of surprise as if he could not believe he had asked that. But then his smile and the sharpness in his eyes returned. He tilted his head. "It's cool and safe, and I promise not to scare you too terribly much. It would be great fun for both of us. You can call me Corvin."

"Corvin...like—" Oh. Wait. I'd wanted to ask him if Corvin meant "raven." But something in his eyes warned me to stop.

"Like just Corvin, or do you have a last name?"

"I am Corvin of the North Sea. That is all. It's all that's ever needed." A bitter note edged his voice. "And what of you? May I have your name?"

"You may call me Mena." I folded my arms, then shrugged. "To be clear, I'm not giving you my name. You can just call me that. I know you're a fae."

"Aren't you clever? Just as clever as you are pretty." He tilted his head, his voice softening. He swam along the edge of the white stone. Those eyes sliced through me, taking me in, examining me, and evaluating me.

My heart beat faster.

Oof.

I didn't need this. "Well...I need to be leaving. Oh. Salt's bane!" The ship had kept sailing—of course it had—and the rope I'd swung out on had almost slipped back into the water.

He straightened in the water, glancing from me and then back over his shoulder. "What's wrong?"

I scooped up the knotted rope before it could slide all the way off the rock. There were only a few hand lengths left and then a little more as I unknotted the lower portion to give myself more slack. This didn't have to be hard unless I got delayed. The one thing I didn't want was to swim and drag along in the water. There were sea monsters other than Corvin out there, and I'd be easy prey.

He followed the line of my gaze back to the ship. A rich chuckle followed. "I don't think this otter rescue of yours turned out according to plan."

I sniffed, narrowing my eyes at him. "Nothing in life goes to plan."

"It's why I never plan anything. What're you going to do now? Are you going to swim?" His smile turned more playful.

More of the white stone islands dotted the sea. The waters were so calm and the winds so still, meaning there were even more of the stone columns revealed today than usual. With the dwarves using their wheeled contraptions to propel the ship forward, I didn't have much time before the ship's steady pace took it beyond the rope's length and I'd have no choice but to swim.

"If you'd like, I could always carry you back," he offered with a sly smile.

Heat flared from my core straight to my face at the thought of being in his arms, all pressed up against his muscular chest and feeling his breath against my cheek. How dare he. "No," I said as flatly as I could.

He stifled a laugh as I fastened the wooden spoon back on the clip at my side. I ignored him pointedly. He obviously wasn't going to be helpful. I then climbed the stone spire at the center of my island and formed my new plan.

The next stone island was a bit farther of a jump, but it was doable. Gripping the rope, I leaped.

The cool, salty air whipped past my face. I landed with a solid thunk on the edge, the impact jarring me through.

While it didn't hurt now, I'd probably be feeling this in the morning.

Squinting, I lifted my hand up and peered at the path ahead. This was the tricky bit, especially with the *Seaforger's Pride* steadily moving forward and ever tugging at the rope. I'd need to jump to the island to the right and then two forward before I could start moving directly ahead. Depending on the distance, I might have to move out to the right again.

I chewed the inside of my lip.

Corvin swam along beside me, watching my every move. His arms slid through the water with practiced grace, a small smirk tugging at his lips. "Thinking, thinking. You know, I never really thought those dwarf ships could move all that fast in doldrum-afflicted waters. Those wooden wheels they run in below deck to power the propellers aren't all that fast. But it might prove a little too fast for you, darling."

Scoffing, I hurried to the edge, then hopped to the island on the right.

Oops!

My heel scraped the water. I swung my arms out and staggered forward. "Stop trying to distract me."

He swam alongside me and circled the tiny rock island. "I bet they'd send a boat out for you. I could swim back and tell them you're out here if you don't trust being in my arms."

"Just stop. I don't need your help." I glared at him as he circled the island again. His long strokes showed off his lean, muscled form, and somehow his hair remained fluffy and curly.

"I'm impressed you didn't just jump into the water. I scared most of the predators down deep, but that heavy thudding and thunking coming from your ship will draw them back up." He trailed his arms lazily through the water. One of the waves lapped against his back, brushing over his hair. After it receded though, his hair was still light and dry. Fae magic maybe.

The otter popped up beside him and nuzzled him, squeaking and chirping. He glanced down at it and grinned. "Tagger really does appreciate you being so eager to help him. Even if he did steal your crossbow."

I wrinkled my nose at him. "You're both horrid."

Tagger splashed in the water and then nuzzled up along Corvin's neck. The otter started grooming him behind the ears, chirping and trilling. No sign of the crossbow. That one smaller forepaw didn't seem to hold him back from his grooming either.

Did the poor fellow have a hard time—no!

No. I wasn't going to get distracted worrying about some little otter that stole my weapon.

Corvin snickered, his voice still melodic but much lower now. "You took that personally, didn't you? If it's any consolation, Tagger likes you. I can tell." Scratching the otter between the ears, he gave me a crooked smile. "He just didn't appreciate you trying to shoot me. He's very protective. Though I do understand why you misunderstood what was happening with Tagger and me. We were just playing."

Huffing, I leaped to the next stone island.

This time I landed neatly on the balls of my feet. The impact still rattled up through me. Ugh.

I adjusted my grip on the knotted rope and looped the strand around my arm to keep it from trailing as I gathered more slack. "Well, lucky you."

No one was protective of me. No one even noticed I was gone. No one would notice I was missing from the ship for at least a couple more hours. Maybe not even until dinnertime arrived and there was no stew and biscuits. And then it wouldn't even be Mama who noticed I was gone. It'd be a crewmember.

My insides twisted, and I tried to push those thoughts away. They weren't helpful.

With a soft grunt, I headed toward the edge and leaped onto the next island. This time I had to scurry around to avoid snagging the rope on the stone spire.

"Well, well," Corvin said, his bright-green eyes half shaded. "Look at you. Just as clever as you are beautiful. I'm half tempted to carry you off right now and let all the problems that may come sort themselves out."

"You stay away from me, shifter fae," I muttered, shooting him a glare. "You and your thieving otter."

"So salty." He tsked as he swam alongside me. Tagger gave a responding trill, managing to be adorable despite his reprehensible acts. "You know that glow in your cheeks from the rage is absolutely adorable. It'd be so easy for me to scoop you up."

"Try it, and I'll kill you with my spoon." I shot him another glare as I adjusted the rope and then leaped forward onto the island to the right.

"Really? With your spoon? How do you kill someone with a spoon?"

I cut my eyes back at him. "Don't push it, shifter."

He tipped his head back and laughed at this. "Oh, chilled waters preserve us, you're a feisty one, aren't you? Why aren't they sending a boat out to get you?" He swam to the other side of the stone island and peeked over the edge of the stone at me. He waggled his eyebrows. "If you were mine, I wouldn't let you out of my home. Or my sight."

Shaking my head, I crossed over the stone island. "Enough. I don't know what you're trying to charm me to do, but it isn't going to work. I'm never going to go with you to your lair. I'm not yours. And I don't think your otter is cute." I leaped onto the next stone circle.

He shot up out of the water as I sailed forward and brushed his clawed fingers over my ankle.

A sharp tingle spasmed up my leg.

I yelped as my feet struck the stone. Spinning around, I glared. "What did you do that for?"

"What did I do?" He gave me an innocent smile that did not reach his eyes. He lifted his arms in a playful shrug. Tagger splashed in the water around him, clapping his paws.

I shook my head at him and padded to the edge of the stone island. "You are—oh!" I jumped back as he zipped in front of me, his bright eyes sparking with mischief. His hand nearly caught my bare ankle again before I darted to the middle of the stone island. What was wrong with him? Was he trying to pull me in?

His voice dipped lower. "Why won't you let me carry you to safety, darling? You know, I make a far better friend than I do an enemy. And you'd fit in my arms so perfectly." He propped his chin up on his palm, his elbow braced against the stone.

I gave him a wide berth as I adjusted my grip.

"Just stay away, all right? I don't want you touching me."

His grin pulled in a crooked slash of white. "Really?"

I unhooked the spoon from the clip at my side and brandished it. "I'm not afraid to hit you in your human form."

He cut his eyes up at me, his grin broadening. "Oh, I'm terrified."

I moved as far as I could away from him, hooked the spoon back on, and prepared to jump. As I launched myself again, he swept forward and ran his hand underneath my feet.

I yelped, the tickling sensation enough to make me flail. "Stop that!" I shouted at him. My fingers clutched at the coarse stone spire, and I tugged on the rope instinctively. One foot brushed the cool waves.

He fluttered his fingers at me as he sank back in the waters, that big grin of his still there. "Aren't you having fun?"

"No." I adjusted my skirt and fixed the soft leggings underneath. As I reached the opposite side of the stone island, I peered out, searching for any threats. The cold waters below were so deep I couldn't even hope to see the bottom. But the relative stillness today meant I could see some of the depth both here and beneath the ship.

As if my thoughts had summoned it, a dark form swept beneath the ship, lithe and sinuous.

Another moved in the distance.

Salt's bane. My stomach churned. The longer I looked, the more I saw.

A side fin cut through the water as one of the sea monsters skimmed the surface and then dove down again. Waves rippled out from it.

"The creatures of the deep love that dwarven racket," Corvin said as he swam back in front of me. "If you had just jumped in, you'd have gotten snatched up like a baby sea turtle in a gull's path on hatching day. But now you've got me curious. How are you going to get from here to your ship?" He tilted his head, his expression sharp but playful. "You must be planning on tying that rope to one of the stone columns and then shimmying across. But you know…that means you're going to be suspended over open waters for a bit. If you fall in, you're dead. And if one of them gets curious about you, well—what's to keep them from snapping a little snack like you out of the air? I bet you'd taste delicious."

I glared at him. "Do you have a point?"

He grinned, eyes half shaded, his eyelashes thick and gorgeous. "I could help you. All you have to do is put your arms around my neck and let me carry you to safety. None of these monsters will cross me. They know exactly what I am."

The way he said that with the glint in his eyes reminded

me without a doubt he was as much a predator as those creatures of the deep. Even if he was gorgeous and had an
incredible smile. Any offer of help masked his true
intentions.

"Come on." He leaned up on the stone. Tagger mimicked
his pose, chirping. "I won't let you drown or fall. You have
my word. Just trust me enough to whisk you over to your
ship."

I narrowed my eyes at him as I adjusted my grip. "Fae like
you always have something else in mind. There's no way I'm
ever trusting you." Sweat rolled down the back of my neck
and my arms, itching all the way. My bare feet ached a little
as I finally reached one of the stone islands that was now
ahead of the ship.

So close and yet so far. I halted next to the stone spire, the
rope snug in my hands. The length swung between me and
the *Seaforger's Pride*, the other end securely fastened on the
post beyond the railing on the ship.

Corvin just laughed. "You won't make it halfway before
you're begging me to help you, darling."

Setting my jaw, I strode over to the stone spire. "Don't bet
on it, shifter fae."

INFURIATING

othing motivated me more than someone telling me I couldn't do something. Even when I was trying to be practical, it was hard to resist the temptation to prove someone wrong and shove it in their faces. Especially when they were so smug and teasing like Corvin.

I adjusted the rope and then secured it to the stone spire, using the technique Hosvir had shown me. He'd said these ropes were woven with magic to make them more secure and responsive.

While I knew magic existed, I'd never been sure whether that was an exaggeration on his part. Here's hoping it wasn't.

I tested it. The rope held fast. But as the ship continued forward, it would slowly draw along the knot while holding tension so long as no one untied it. If it was loosened though, it'd start to slip. I gave it another firm tug.

Corvin continued to watch, that big smirking grin on his face. He slid his arms through the water as he rose and fell with the waves. "This will be fun. Do you really think that rope is going to hold?"

"It's enchanted. It won't come loose until I give the command word." The last part was a lie. But hopefully one that would keep him from messing with it. I glanced over the waters as I gripped the coarse-fibered rope tighter. Adjusting my skirt, I climbed up the stone spire and set myself against the rope. It bobbed and swayed beneath my weight.

My stomach twisted. I steadied myself, drawing in slow breaths.

I could do this.

I really could.

Then—slowly—I stretched out over the rope, rolled under it, wrapped my knees over it, crossed my ankles, and gripped it with my hands.

My heart raced faster as I hung there. Hand over hand, I crawled along out over the water.

The waves rolled and splashed against the little island. A faint mist of salt spray caressed my face.

Corvin gave an amused grunt, his eyes half hooded. "Having fun yet, darling?"

"Why don't you show me how long you can hold your breath and go under?" I cast him a dark glare.

A laugh answered me. He flicked his long yellow-and-green striped tail and swept beneath me. "You don't really want me to leave. What'll you do when your strength gives out? I've got to be here to catch you when you fall."

Salt's bane, he was aggravating. "I'm not falling."

"Yet."

I continued to monkey-crawl along the rope. The itching fibers grated along my callused hands, uncomfortable but manageable. My skirt rode up, revealing the pale-blue leggings underneath. Thank goodness for those leggings though because they kept my legs from getting scratched as bad as my hands. My bare feet pressed along the taut rope and helped me push along.

Hand over hand. Pulling and tugging myself forward.

The creaking and shifting of the rope beneath my grasp unnerved me.

How much time before the ship pulled ahead and drew the rope's length out from the knot?

It had felt so much easier before I was out here over the ocean with who knew what lurking beneath me.

Sweat formed on my brow. I hooked my elbow over the rope and dashed my free hand over my face to wipe the sweat away. The rope bobbed. I wasn't nearly as high as I wanted. But it would increase in height as I neared the ship.

Corvin swam along beneath with a lazy backstroke, keeping pace with me. "Why is such a beautiful woman out here all alone anyway? Is there anyone out here protecting you?"

I set my jaw. "I take care of myself."

That was how it had been even before Mama and I left to find Erryn, my sister. Now it was even more true.

I dragged myself along the underside of the rope. Already my arms and legs burned. At least I was strong enough now.

I glanced out toward the ship. That dark reptilian shape sliced under the ship again, gliding like a shadow. It hadn't come closer to me. Or maybe it was more that it didn't want to come closer to Corvin.

As if he guessed my thoughts, he flung a handful of water up in the air. The droplets rained down on me. One rolled into my eye, making it sting. "You realize how precarious your situation is, don't you, darling?"

Rolling my eyes, I continued, gritting my teeth. "Do you realize how annoying you are?"

More laughter followed, along with another splash. His hand made a loud slap against the water the second time.

I clutched the rope tighter, shaking my head to clear my eyes. "You're behaving like such a child!"

"Really?" He swam a little ahead of me. "You know, I'm curious about this magical rope of yours. Dwarf made, I'm assuming. That's what they generally use. They don't have a weight limit, do they?"

Grumbling, I kept crawling. This was taking so much longer than I'd expected.

Another splash sent droplets of water raining down on me. I cringed, then yelped as the rope suddenly dipped, tipping me down headfirst.

I twisted my head to see Corvin hanging on the rope in front of me, suspended by only one arm.

My eyes widened. "What are you doing?"

With a casual wink, he lowered and then lifted himself, flexing his muscles with the movement. His long, sleek eel tail remained partially submerged in the water. "Now this is remarkable. It doesn't feel like the rope is strained even a little bit."

"Get off," I growled through gritted teeth, clenching my hands and knees tighter around the rope as I hung upside down.

"The rope can easily hold us both, darling." He continued to hold himself in the air, his tail sweeping back and forth in slow strokes. Then, with a tilt of his head, he ran the claws of his free hand along the fibers of the rope. "I don't think it'd be easy to cut either."

The rope creaked a little more, though not threatening to break. But the ship was pulling ahead. I had to move faster. "No. You can't cut it. It won't work," I lied.

"Pity for me. Bonus for you." He released his hand. That same smirking smile still on his face, he plunged back down under the waters.

I quickened my pace. My hands and ankles burned against the rope, but still, I twisted around just enough to check on where he was. Corvin had become nothing more than a dark form beneath the waters. He circled down with the easy grace of an apex predator before vanishing into the shadows. Tagger paddled toward the stone island where my rope was tethered.

Another hand's length forward.

If I could keep up this pace, I'd be back aboard the ship and safe in less than ten minutes. I could last that long, right?

"I think you're moving slower now. Are you getting tired, darling?" Corvin's voice sounded a little farther ahead now.

There he was again. The smug bastard.

A tremor in the rope snapped my attention back to the island.

Tagger stood on the top of the spire, sniffing the knot. He placed one paw on it.

Was he going to climb out on the rope with me? My muscles tightened. "No, it's not safe!" Six feet was a long way to fall for such a little otter, and that one bad paw of his might make his balance quite poor.

"Oh, so you do care?" Corvin sang out. "I knew it."

"Oh, shut up!" I adjusted my grip as I forced myself forward. "I don't care." That didn't mean I wanted to see the little creature hurt. Life had enough brutality as it was.

Tagger chirped, sitting up on the edge of the pillar.

I shook my head at him as I continued along. "Both of you, just leave me alone, all right?"

Another tremor passed through the rope, and I started to sink.

What?

I wrenched my gaze back in time to see Tagger fiddling with the knot and sliding more rope through.

"No!" My eyes widened. "No, no, no! Bad otter. Bad Tagger!"

Tagger continued to work at the rope, causing it to lower closer and closer to the water.

I clung there, upside down, hair swinging in the breeze. My mauve skirt hung about my hips. Lovely. My face was almost in line with Corvin's now.

Corvin grinned and leaned forward.

I wrinkled my nose. "I said stay away from me."

"So you did. But here you are." He grinned, rising up from the water so that we were eye to eye. Waggling his eyebrows, he brushed the tip of his forefinger's claw against my nose. "What if I were to kiss you right now?"

I glared at him, then seized the spoon from the clip at my side and struck him on the forehead. "I said no."

He laughed at this but slid back. "It's a good thing you're so entertaining. Otherwise—" His hand darted up and brushed against the ends of my auburn hair.

I smacked his hand with the spoon again. "Do you understand what no means?"

"I've heard it means you want to extend the game." He swam out a little farther and then circled back, his eyes sparkling.

I was barely three feet above the water now. It was going to be a much steeper climb once I reached the ship. "I want you to leave me alone," I said as sternly as I could. "Tell your otter to stop."

He flashed me an even bigger smile, then leaned back and whistled. "Don't drop her in the water, Tagger. Let's see what she can manage on her own." He cut his gaze back to me. "I have to admit, darling, I really want to see if you can manage the rest of the way. You're stronger than you look."

"And you're patronizing and infuriating." More sweat and salt water rolled down my neck and arms.

"Only when I'm right. Which I always am."

I grumbled as I continued along. A gorgeous man finally

wanted to talk to me, but he was a fae intent on tormenting me. Sounded about right, actually. How dare he. How dare he be so attractive and so horrible at the same time!

He splashed his tail up out of the water, sending a spray of salty water over me.

"Oh!" I gritted my teeth.

"Does that help you cool off in this heat?" he asked with teasing sweetness.

I looked at him and froze. He was half out of the water, gripping the rope with one hand as he blocked my path. "This is now a toll line. Pay the toll, and I'll let you pass."

I pulled the spoon free again. "Move, or I'll whack your fingers."

"Has anyone ever told you that spoons aren't actually weapons, darling?" He laughed as he leaned forward. His fingers grazed my cheek, the claws light and tingling across my skin. "Then again, that does look like a special spoon. I never knew anyone to carry around a wooden spoon with marks like that. What do they say?"

I huffed at him, the spoon still raised in one hand. My left arm ached and burned as I held myself up. "If I tell you, will you get off this rope?"

"I swear it." He batted his eyelashes at me. "What does it say?"

"Salt before pepper makes it better." It was a lie. But he wouldn't know that if he couldn't read runes.

He chuckled darkly. "Oh, darling, I can't even read ordinary common script. But I can read faces. So now I'm doubly interested. What does it really say?" His hand cupped my cheek, peering at me as I stared at him upside down.

"Never give up on your dreams." I set my jaw. That wasn't something I'd intended to admit, and even hanging upside down, I couldn't hide the bitterness in my voice. I felt vulnerable, and I hated it as much as I hated the advice on the spoon and cherished the kind souls who'd given it to me.

"Such rage." The teasing faded from his voice as he leaned closer to me, his emerald-green eyes half shaded. "Why?"

"Because dreams are pointless, unless what you really want are opportunities for disappointment."

His eyes widened briefly as he cocked his head. "Well… that went dark. You really think that, darling?"

The note of sincerity in his voice startled me. I hung there and stared at him, forcing my gaze to remain hard. "You think it's not true?"

His expression wavered, a look of contemplative sadness reaching his eyes. "Hadn't thought about it for a long time."

"Probably for the best."

"Then why are you so determined to get back on the ship? What has your fires burning so strong?" he asked, softer now.

"My mother and I are trying to find my sister." I had said this so many times over the past years. Heard the story told even more times than I had spoken it. Watched the life fade from my mother as we gave up everything to find Erryn. "She went missing years ago."

"And you think she's out in this sea?" His eyebrows arched. He continued to hang off the rope, but he didn't pull away or draw closer.

"No. We're trying to get to the oracle who lives beyond the North Sea in the Shining Pass."

"That oracle is a fraud." He scoffed, suggesting visiting her was the most ridiculous thing he could imagine.

I bit my tongue, wanting to agree. "Yeah, well, we're going to stop at an island near the boundary first. Apparently, there are a pair of grounded staircases with portals at the end that Mama thinks could be used to shorten the trip. Maybe she'll find something else to help. But what we do is our own business, all right? I didn't ask you for your advice. So unless you can tell me where my sister is or how to find her, I'd appreciate it if you'd just shut up and get out of the way."

"Hmmm." He narrowed his eyes at me as his voice hummed low. "Intriguing." Then he released his hold and dropped into the sea. His body knifed under the water with careless ease.

I breathed with relief and then resumed my climb, my muscles shaking and stiff. My body protested with each inch I gained, but at least I was over halfway there.

Corvin's dark form disappeared into the deeper shadows of the water, followed by Tagger.

A pang of unease struck me.

Something else was watching me.

Urging myself forward, I continued my climb. Less than fifteen feet away now. The rope angled up more, and it eased forward as the ship pulled ahead. But even if I fell in, I was so close—wait.

Movement caught my eye.

Oh, salt's bane!

The shadow of the reptilian creature near the ship circled before the bow and started toward me.

Damn it!

My heart clenched. Whether a water dragon or a sea croc or something else, I had to get to the ship. I gritted my teeth and pulled myself forward faster.

The shadowy creature drew closer, its sinuous movements hypnotic but deadly. As it turned its triangular head to the side, the glint of a red eye gleamed up through the waters. Then, graceful as a deadly swan, it ducked its head and charged down.

Damn the beast!

I dragged myself along faster.

It was going to breach.

The barnacled side of the ship loomed before me, so close

and yet much too far for me to make it in time. The water lapped at the glistening wood.

Come on, faster. Faster!

I ground my teeth together. The water had made the rope slicker.

The dark shape of the sea monster below shot up. Its heavy jaws parted.

UNNOTICED

*W*ith a frightened shriek, I clutched the rope with my knees and ankles and dragged myself forward. I moved so fast the fibers cut my palms and legs.

It stung. But those teeth slicing into my flesh would be worse.

Dread slicked through me. I couldn't move fast enough.

The monster lunged out of the water, seizing the rope as it rose up in the air. The sturdy fibers were nothing against the razor-sharp teeth of the creature, and the rope snapped as soon as it pulled taut.

A gasp choked me—then I crashed into the salty waves, clinging to the knotted rope. Cold waters rushed around me, filling my nose and my mouth. My hearing went dull, my mouth sharp with the salty tang of the sea and fear. The force almost ripped the rope from my hands. Kicking furiously, I fought to reach the surface far above and forced my eyes open.

The salt water stung my eyes, but the enormous dark form of the sea monster filled my vision. It was sinking back down now. Its glowing red eye homed in on me.

No!

I kicked and clutched, clawing along the rope as my only lifeline.

Another dark form shot up. Longer. Serpentine. An enormous yellow-and-green striped eel with ferocious eyes and massive jaws. The bright-green eyes opened but focused on the sea monster.

Corvin.

He'd been a thorn in my side, but I wasn't going to pretend I wasn't happy to see him now. Even if that eel form was utterly terrifying.

He struck the reptilian sea monster in the stomach with his head. The sea monster let out a vibrating croak that filled my ears despite the pressure of the water.

I emerged from the water and gasped for breath, clutching the rope tight. The ship was only a few lengths away. Kicking, I started to swim, keeping my grip on the rope tight.

The sea monster dove down again, its dark shape vanishing, a trail of blood spiraling up from it.

My hand struck the side of the ship, and I gasped with relief. The salt water burned my cuts and scrapes, but tears of joy rolled down my cheeks.

Almost there!

Corvin swam to the surface as I slowly scaled the side of the ship. "You didn't let go," he said, a note of respect in his voice. "Disappointed as I am that I didn't get to hold you, I've got to admit you impressed me, Mena."

I gulped in another breath. My whole body ached, and my clothes weighed me down. It took every ounce of strength and focus for me to drag myself up.

Water ran out of my skirt and bodice. The ship rocked in the waves, and the steady, thudding knocks of the wheels in the hold filled my ears and vibrated against my chest. "Glad —I—could be—amusing, you—son of a—scallop."

His uproarious laugh reached my ears.

Nope. Not looking back at him. All that mattered was getting up.

"Glad to see my clever darling isn't losing her spirit just because she took a dip in the sea." He pressed his hand against the hull and stared up at me. Admiration glinted in his eyes along with the hunger.

"I'm not yours," I sputtered. "I'm my own woman."

"You most certainly are." He grinned. "And I wouldn't have it any other way."

My muscles strained as I reached the top. The heavy beat of the wheels and gears below deck seemed louder. I flung my arm over the first ledge and hauled myself to the railing.

Finally!

Corvin chuckled below. "You're a strange one, Mena. And strange things will follow you wherever you go."

Huffing, I heaved myself over the railing and collapsed in a puddle of water and fabric. I then twisted around, staggered up, and leaned against the railing. "As long as you aren't the one following me, I can manage that," I said as gruffly as I could.

He laughed heartily. "I can't guarantee that, darling, now can I?"

"Listen." I scrubbed my hand across my face. "Thank you for helping me with the sea monster. But I don't owe you a thing, understand?"

He grinned as he swam alongside the ship. "One might say saving your life counts as you owing me something of my choosing. Unless you've got a reason that you wouldn't owe me."

"I wouldn't have needed help if you hadn't been toying with me." I gulped in another burning breath. My knees felt like they were about to give out. "And I did try to save your otter."

"Yes, you did, clever girl." That smile of his went crooked again and made my stomach twist. He tapped his hand to his brow. "Of course, all this would have been entirely unnecessary if you'd just let me carry you in my arms to your ship."

"Not going to happen."

"Fair enough. I might not have been able to resist the temptation to keep you." That sharp, hungry look of his intensified. Then he shook his head. Somehow his curls were still dry and perfect, half covering his eyes. "I wish you all the best in the search to find your sister. Perhaps we'll meet again soon, and I'll carry you off yet."

With that, he dove down.

I started to draw back when a sharp chirping and trilling sounded at the hull. Glancing back down, I couldn't resist the smile that sprang to my lips.

Tagger bobbed in the waves on his back, the other end of the rope in his hands. It must have come free from the stone spire and fallen out of the sea monster's mouth.

Quirking my mouth up, I dragged the ragged end of the rope toward Tagger. The magic woven into the rope sprang to life, sending up a bright yet musty scent of salt, straw, flax, and leather. It glowed for a moment as the strands combined once more, allowing the rope to become whole.

"Thank you," I said with a small smile. "You actually are cute. And I guess you are loyal. I can't fault you for that."

Tagger chattered, his long, white whiskers twitching. Then he dove beneath the waves. Corvin's shadowy form remained below as if waiting. As the otter neared him, he lingered a moment longer.

Was he watching me?

I shouldn't be looking at him. It wasn't as if I wanted to

encourage him in this sort of behavior. He'd been entirely inappropriate.

And I wasn't interested in that sort of thing.

So why couldn't I stop staring?

And why did the skin along the back of my neck prickle and my arms goosebump?

I tried to swallow. The salt water had left my throat aching and sore, and the struggle had drained my body of its strength.

That's why I had to lean here and stare down at the sea.

And he remained there for two breaths longer until he at last turned and whisked down into the darkness below.

Salt's bane.

What was wrong with me?

I forced myself to step back, my knees still shaky. Water sluiced off my body in rivulets as I staggered across the deck to the staircase and my cabin.

Not a thing had changed onboard the ship in my absence. A few of the dwarves tended to their posts farther up on the ship and below deck, though clearly no one was really watching the sea. Thank the Creator nothing had tried to attack us. Whatever charms they used for safety had their complete confidence.

With the relative quiet and calm and the early autumn sun, there wasn't as much for the dwarven sailors to do when it wasn't their shift to run in the wheels. Most were probably resting, including the sentry in the crow's nest.

I sighed. No one really noticed anything I did unless it involved food, which was a blessing and a curse.

I washed up, then changed into a clean dark-blue dress with an apron. It was almost the middle of the afternoon.

Mik, the ship's cook, greeted me with a firm nod and a rough grunt. He wasn't much for talking. But he had been pleased to have someone else onboard to help with the meals. Especially when it came to chopping the vegetables and deboning the fish. He'd laughed at me the first time I'd asked for tweezers to pluck the pin bones, but then he'd gruffly acknowledged I hadn't done half bad.

That and requests for specific types of stews or dishes were the highest of compliments I got.

It wasn't so bad.

But the way that Corvin had teased and flirted with me... my cheeks heated now as much as they had when I was facing him.

It had been ages since someone said I was pretty.

Honestly, it'd probably be ages more before anyone would again. If they ever did.

Why was I wasting time on this?

I checked the lentils to make sure they were ready and then dumped them into the large iron stew pot. Then I checked on the other ingredients to search for anything that was on its last legs. Some of the ears of corn needed to be used, so I shucked and cut them. Turmeric and leeks were a good fit for this as well. Plus a little ginger.

It was cozy and calm within the galley. I chopped with precision, though my thoughts kept drifting back to Corvin. Mik didn't try to engage me in conversation. He didn't speak often, even outside the galley. Unless it was to tell me about a chore that needed tending.

I always handled it, no matter what it was. And at least he was polite about it. Especially considering he didn't have to be. Really, most of the dwarves on the *Seaforger's Pride* were nice enough, provided you didn't mind bluntness and lots of huffing. Their hunting otters—easily as big as they were—were much more fun. Larger than hunting dogs but just as friendly, some as big as lions and even smarter. When the running wheels weren't going, the dwarves had to barricade the galley if the hunting otters weren't down in their berths. The massive brown-furred creatures loved stew as much as their own meals, and they would happily lick any pot clean.

Tagger would probably do the same. And he was so much smaller and faster, so he'd probably be harder to stop.

Wait—why was I thinking about Tagger?

I shook my head.

Just because I didn't belong here didn't mean I should be thinking about a shifter fae and his troublesome otter.

I had work to do. That's where my attention needed to be.

The afternoon passed relatively quickly, even though I couldn't put Corvin out of my mind. I kept wondering what would have happened if I had agreed to go with him.

A shudder passed through me.

Nothing good.

Of course not.

What good ever came of a human running off with a fae?

None.

Nothing but heartbreak.

A fae was the reason my sister had vanished. At least if the rumors were true.

Emotion knotted in my throat, tears stinging my eyes.

It felt like we'd been looking for Erryn for forever, and yet I could remember the first day she'd gone missing with painful clarity. The panic in Mama's dark-grey eyes. The cold, greasy ball of fear that formed in my stomach. The creak of the floor as we paced and talked. The rumors that swirled about the village—that Erryn had taken a cursed fae bargain and been whisked away.

Tears threatened to spill down my cheeks.

After all this time, it was hard for me to believe that Erryn was still alive. Despite being selfish, Erryn was smart. She'd have found a way to get in touch with us. And there hadn't been a word out of her or about her beyond vague rumors of others who had gone missing thanks to roving glamouring fae.

That hadn't kept Mama from devoting her life to finding Erryn and researching every bit of arcane magic and lore that she thought might help her bring Erryn home.

Except none of this would help Erryn.

If I was honest with myself, the only reason I was still doing this was because I didn't want to abandon Mama. If I didn't take care of her, who would?

I ladled some of the steaming stew into a wooden bowl and picked up a couple slices of bread warm from the oven. Mik's salt and honey rye bread was good plain or with butter. Dinner in hand, out the door I went.

The first few weeks on the ship, I'd struggled to keep my footing. But now I could have walked across the deck with a full bowl of steaming tomato soup in a white dress and been mostly all right.

I found Mama in the study adjacent to the captain's quarters. That's where Mama usually was these days, hunched over maps and books as she struggled to pull any scrap of meaning from ancient texts that had no bearing on anything we were doing except for the fact they were about fae who stole humans or similar topics like portals. Lately she'd been obsessed with stairways in the air, the grounded and ungrounded ones and all their dangers and possibilities those portals held.

The study itself was small and dimly lit by a single oil lamp set in a rotating case and hung from the ceiling by wires. A little flame flickered, providing a surprising amount of light considering its size. The walls were lined with shelves that came up to my waist, and then the walls were plastered with maps, their edges yellowed and curled in. Old books and cases of scrolls filled most of the shelves, along with a few dark-stained chests. Precious little light flowed through the single porthole, but a bit of a breeze eked in. The heavy, musty scent of old paper and older leather with the strong scent of sailor's tobacco and a musky cologne that hadn't been used in ages filled my lungs. It left a dry but not unpleasant taste in my mouth.

A large table sat in the center of the room, fastened to the floor. Stacks of papers and books filled most of it, but a shiny brown teapot sat on the right corner near Mama's right hand along with a squat cup of now-cold tea.

Captain Hosvir had been smitten with Mama since the day we walked into the shipyard. Not that he would admit it to me. But he seemed to love talking with her and had many questions about these portals. Sometimes I wondered if there was something on this island that he wanted to find as well. He wasn't here at the moment, but that tea set was one he'd brought out on our second day at sea. He'd excused it by saying sometimes he enjoyed a nice cup of tea himself. And slowly that had turned into a mid-afternoon exchange between Mama and the captain. If Mama wasn't too busy.

There was no sign of the captain's cup, and Mama was especially focused on the pages in front of her. The tea in her cup hadn't been touched either. Nor had the little slice of seedcake that had slid off the plate and partially under a large faded volume.

Sighing, I stepped inside. "Mama," I said, holding the plate of bread and stew. "I know you haven't eaten today. So you need to eat dinner. All right?"

Mama nodded without looking up. Her thinning auburn hair was now more than half silver, and her eyeglasses sat low on her nose. One lens had cracked months ago. A simple enough fix, except she wouldn't spend a cent on anything that didn't bring her closer to finding Erryn. Her ragged green shawl had been drawn up over her bony shoulders and wrapped tight around her frail frame. She'd become so much more haggard and worn over the past few years, shrinking to little more than a shell of herself. Some days she refused to eat at all. Months and months of fruitless searching had carved deep lines in her face and sapped her strength and vitality.

I cleared my throat. "Mama," I said, louder this time. "I have to insist. You need to actually eat something."

"Just put it down," Mama said without looking up.

I moved the books aside and set the steaming bowl of stew down. The fragrant scent of cod, corn, lentils, and spices filled the air, accented by the warm yeasty scent of honey-and-salt rye bread.

She didn't turn her head or glance at it.

I placed my hand on her shoulder. "Mama."

She shook her head. "I'll get to it when I get a chance. I need to focus. There's something here—something that might give us the answer. I've translated the proper runes for activation. We may be able to use it."

Unlikely. Mama had learned many incredible things, but none of them had ever really helped to find Erryn. After we reached this oracle and dealt with the sorrow of learning yet again that there was nothing to help us find Erryn, I needed to talk with Mama about settling down again. We couldn't keep on doing this. But that meant Mama had to make it until then.

"Mama," I said again, firmer this time. "Have you eaten anything since yesterday? You didn't touch your tea. You need to eat something."

Another shake of the head, her focus on the page before her and the possible connections she was drawing from texts that had nothing to do with Erryn.

I squared my shoulders. "I'm not leaving until you take at least a bite of stew. You're being ridiculous." I said it with a tone, knowing that that would at least get a reaction from Mama.

Oh, did it ever.

Her gaze snapped to me, her eyes watery and bloodshot from hours of poring over texts. "You think it's ridiculous for me to look for your sister? Don't you care about Erryn, Philomena?"

I kept my chin up. "I do. But I also care about you. And you're going to be worthless or dead if you don't eat something."

"Don't take that tone with me, young lady. I said to leave it here," Mama said, her tone sharpening. "You don't need to patronize me. I will eat when I need to eat."

"Except you don't! You're so focused on finding Erryn that you won't even spend fifty coppers to get your lenses fixed." The words were sliding out, and I regretted it almost as soon as I realized it was happening. But it was too late. I kept my gaze steady, already regretting my next words. "It's been years. We may never find her! We can't keep living like this."

"She could still be alive." Mama hugged the shawl tighter around herself. Her thin brows pinched together. "Nothing is more important than finding Erryn, Philomena Ophelia Lyster. I would have thought you would understand by now. Your sister has not been found. We do not rest until she is found. We cannot give up on her! She's counting on us."

I gritted my teeth, my muscles tensing. There was so much I wanted to say about this, but I choked it all down to focus on what was important. "That doesn't mean you should starve yourself. If you really care about finding Erryn, the least you can do is eat."

"Don't you dare disrespect your sister's name like that." Mama's voice shook. Her face had gone pale. "I—I can't believe how callous you are about her sometimes."

I bit my tongue. Arguing further would make it worse. "Just one bite. All right? Then I'll leave."

Mama's mouth pinched. She picked up the piece of seed-cake, tore off a small piece, and placed it in her mouth. "There."

A bitter taste filled my mouth. I forced a smile though. "Good enough." It was hard not to see Mama's decision to eat the seedcake and not my stew as personal. But at least she'd eaten something.

Mama mumbled something under her breath as she sat back down. She didn't even glance at the bowl of stew.

My heart clenched. Bile rose in the back of my mouth.

Part of me wanted to shove the books off the table and demand Mama take care of herself. If not for me, then for herself or Hosvir.

Instead I drew in a deep breath and strode toward the door. It creaked open easily as if the very wood realized how bad it would be for me to remain in this room. Hand on the door jamb, I hesitated. "I love you, Mama," I forced the words out.

Mama nodded without looking up. "I love you too, sweetheart." Tears ran down her cheeks, a few dropping onto the yellowed pages. She hunched over the scribbled pages.

Some small part of me wanted to tell Mama about Corvin and Tagger and all that had happened. But the words died before I could speak them.

It wasn't the first time something strange had happened to me. I'd just learned not to waste my breath telling Mama about those things. It only left me feeling ignored and sad when I told the whole story and Mama simply nodded or said "mmhmm."

So I left, the words locked tight within my chest.

I didn't eat any dinner that night either. Instead, I went straight to bed. This could not continue.

The doldrums continued over the next two days. We made decent progress with the dwarf wheels below the hold that propelled the ship ever forward, but it was tedious.

I helped with the cooking and cleaning. I even took a turn in one of the wooden wheels, jogging along at a steady pace. A couple of the dwarves operated hand fans that kept the air moving. The dwarves hummed and sang at times to keep the rhythm.

When I went to the quartermaster to tell him what happened with the mini-crossbow and the bolts, he didn't want to hear it. Instead he scolded me for being careless and told me to do better next time. Some of the younger crew members had lost their weapons before this, but this was my first time, and the reprimand stung. It was fair though. I had lost the crossbow.

Nothing drove away the aching sensation that I was missing something important. Each time I went above deck to cool off or rest, I went to the starboard side or the stern where I'd first glimpsed Tagger and peered down.

I was just checking to see if the otter was down there. That was all.

It wasn't like I was actually looking for Corvin.

But if he was there, I might say hello.

Shadows stirred within the deep, circling and watching. Captain Hosvir insisted none of them would attack the ship so long as we stayed on the right side of the boundary. Such caution didn't keep creatures from following in the hopes someone might fall in.

Corvin was dreadful. Horrid.

And charming.

I sighed, propping my fist against my cheek. The waves sloshed against the sides of the ship, the salty spray forming a broad fan.

Back before Erryn had vanished, I'd had friends. Some

worked in the tavern. Others were in the village. They'd have begged me for details about Corvin and teased me relentlessly.

Not having anyone to tell me I was catching feelings for someone took out all the fun of denying it.

Especially when I couldn't hide from the truth.

I probably wasn't falling for Corvin. I was just lonely, and I liked the attention.

I was pathetic.

On the second night, I finished helping Mik clean up the galley from the cod and anchovy stew and then I went to my room, even though it wasn't yet dark.

Tucking the heavy blue blanket around myself, I removed a borrowed book from the drawer. A cookbook with stories from the Tide Breaker Clan. Nothing particularly riveting but comforting nonetheless.

Usually it was enough to make me drowsy.

Tonight, sleep refused to come. Instead, an odd unsettling feeling rose from the pit of my stomach and tightened into my chest.

I rubbed the base of my throat, pondering what it was. Not a pain. Not a disturbance. Just…an awareness.

The impulse intensified.

I needed to get up.

Now.

I strode out into the narrow, wooden hallway. The ship bobbed and rocked, the waves far stronger than in previous days. A couple of the dwarves sat on the stairs, chatting amiably and smoking. They didn't notice me. Neither did the sentry.

I made my way through the hall until I reached the study once more. The oil lamp's soft golden light glowed beneath the door. A stern debate was happening. The captain was not pleased, his rumbling bass so low I struggled to distinguish words.

Then another voice spoke, sharper and deadlier.

That voice.

I knew that voice.

Without knocking, I pressed the door to the study open. My hand gripped the knob to keep the natural rocking of the ship from jarring it further open as I peeked inside.

I froze.

Corvin.

LEANING

*M*ama stood behind Hosvir, her hand at the base of her throat as she stared at Corvin with wide, frightened eyes. Hosvir stood with his burly arms akimbo, his stance strong and his gaze narrowed on Corvin. His iron-grey beard with streaks of red framed his broad features, but worry glinted in one narrowed dark-blue eye.

Corvin—my stomach somersaulted.

Salt's bane, he chilled and heated my blood at once. He stood on the other side of the room, his manner deceptively lazy and languid as he regarded Mama and Hosvir.

He was much taller in his human form than I'd expected. Long and lithe.

Almost like a dancer. Yet deadlier.

His expression was hard, and the unusual yellow-and-green stripes over his face, neck, and hands made his appearance all the more alarming and severe and...beautiful. His hair, though still loose and curled, was pushed back from his face in a more orderly fashion. He wore elegant black garb with accents of a dusky yellow-orange. The fashion was outdated and similar to the older northern traditions, but it was well kept and crisp, the black fabric as rich and dark as if freshly dyed. His boots were oiled and shiny, his posture firm.

"This is your warning," Corvin said. No melody laced his voice, no playfulness danced in his eyes. "But you, Captain, should not require one. You know the purpose of these waters and what lies beyond the boundary. You know as well the agreement. You know how all of this works."

Captain Hosvir remained in his powerful stance. Though he was only a little over five feet tall, he looked strong enough to snap a full-grown man in two. His green-and-indigo kraken tattoo peeked out from the edges of his dark-green coat sleeves. The raging of his pulse along his throat and a flicker in his one good eye were the only real indicators that he was actually afraid. "Aye. I do, and we have not crossed the boundaries."

Corvin's eyebrow flicked upward in contempt. "No, but there's a storm coming. And you're dangerously close. It would take very little to send your vessel over the edge into forbidden waters. Especially when the boundary line shifts. And who is to say how far it will shift? You know the stories."

"We're headed to the Salt Channel. Not the North Sea," Captain Hosvir said gruffly. "We'll navigate it after the storm passes. No one here is trying to get anything past the King of the North Sea."

Mama stepped closer. Her fingers brushed Corvin's arm.

Captain Hosvir's eyes widened. He darted forward with surprising speed and drew Mama back. He whispered something to Mama in a voice so low I couldn't catch it before he placed himself in front of her. Though Mama was a little taller than Hosvir, she seemed much smaller and frailer, her expression now chastened and her shoulders drawn tight.

Corvin's eyes narrowed on her, disgust twitching in his

features. He didn't even seem to notice the captain. "Do not touch me."

"Please. We are only trying to reach the Oracle of the Glass Mountain," Mama said, her voice shaking. "And—and we know of the island near the boundary of the North Sea. It would be faster if you granted us permission to enter the North Sea. We could reach both within a day if you would. Surely the king will understand that we are searching for my youngest—"

"The king has no more mercy than the sea," Corvin growled. "There is neither mercy nor leeway in these requirements. If the boundary line shifts and you are on the wrong side of it, this ship will be destroyed."

"But if you would just speak to him and ask him for his permission so that we could at least visit the island—" Mama tried to reach for him again. Hosvir shushed her, reaching out with his large hand to grip her arm.

Corvin's glare turned icy. "No," he growled.

Mama fell back. She looked as if he'd slapped her. Her chin trembled as she bit back the tears. "My youngest—"

"Means nothing to me and less to the King of the North Sea." The venom and ice in Corvin's voice could not have been any colder.

Mama darted forward, moving around Hosvir. She grabbed at Corvin's arm, her fingers clutching at his sleeve with desperation.

He hissed, pushing her away.

The ship tilted as he did, the books and papers sliding against the ledges of the table. Mama lurched back. Corvin held his ground, glaring at her. She collapsed on the other side of the room as the scrolls rolled out and the books slid away. A pained cry escaped her lips. Had he shoved her?

I sprang forward, slamming the door open. "Don't touch my mother!" My fists clenched.

Reaching the table, I seized the silver precision pencil compass and lifted it like a dagger.

He spun to face me. No alarm rose in his eyes. No concern either. Only delight. The hint of a smile flashed before vanishing into the carved marble of his features.

"Ahh, the stew cook. Come to threaten me with a spoon again, clever girl? Or...a compass, I suppose," he sneered. Yet as he spoke, there was more a note of play than there had been before.

I kept my grip on the pencil compass tight, the silver point glinting in the low lamplight.

"Don't touch him, Philomena," Captain Hosvir called out, his voice rough and low. He knelt beside Mama, his arms around her and holding her close as if she were a wounded bird. "He is one of the enforcers of the King of the North Sea. He cannot be touched unless he initiates it or harms someone here."

"And I have harmed no one here." Corvin spread his arms in a mocking bow, his attention focused wholly on me. "I can see now why you were so anxious to get back to this ship. Obviously you share your mother's focus and her determination to save her *one* daughter."

"Do you know this man?" Mama looked at me with wide, weepy eyes. She tried to stand.

Captain Hosvir's thick grey eyebrows lifted as well, but he returned his attention to Mama, helping her to her feet and checking her for injuries.

I lifted my chin, the compass still gripped in my hand. "Enforcer or not, hurt anyone in my family, and I will hurt you back."

Corvin tilted his head, his gaze narrowing. "You say that as if you've put your words to the test. Intriguing. Maybe you have your own teeth and claws, darling." He smirked as he glanced from me back to Mama. "You must take after your father."

"Why are you here?" I demanded.

"To deliver a message. Which I have done. You have all been warned. Beware of the boundary line and abide by our laws." He tipped his head and strode away. His cloak swirled out behind him with a dramatic snap.

I set the pencil compass down on the table next to the little book Mama had been working on. My fingers ached from gripping it so tight. "How can a boundary line shift?"

Mama burst into sobs, her whole body shaking. "The island may be our only hope for finding Erryn in time. We have to do something! We have to. I know my translations are correct. If we can access the island and reach the staircase there, I can test it. We might not even have to continue sailing. We can look through all of the staircases and see if there are any signs. It could fix everything!"

Captain Hosvir kept his arm around her. He gave her shoulder a gentle pat. "It'll be all right. We'll find another way, dove. There's never only one way to do anything, hmm?"

Mama shook her head, tears still streaming down her cheeks. Her eyes were bloodshot, and she couldn't even stand up straight. "We can't afford any delays! It's been too long already. Every second counts!"

My mouth pinched. As angry as I got with Mama, I hated seeing her cry. She couldn't be reasoned with when she was like this. "We'll figure something out." I spun on my heel and chased after Corvin.

Corvin's footsteps rang in my mind. They were heavy and strong, half the pace of the beat of my heart.

I turned the corner and spotted him striding away.

"You're just going to leave?" I spat the words out like rotted food. "You threaten us, almost hit my mother, and then decide to leave?"

Corvin turned to face me, eyes blazing and hungry once

more as his gaze ran over me. The smirk had turned cruel. "I did not strike your mother. She tried to grab me. I pushed her off. The ship took care of the rest. But that's not why you came chasing after me, is it?" His eyes hooded. "There's something you want from me."

My breath caught in my throat. Thank the Creator for those infernal stripes and vibrant colors or else I'd have been completely lost in his presence. I lifted my chin. "Listen, I don't know much about what lies in these waters. But, besides the oracle, apparently there's an island my mother wants to visit. She says it will help us find my sister. Maybe we'll find some sort of closure. I'm not asking it as a favor. We'd be more than willing to pay. Just name the price."

"There is no price," he responded.

"Fine." I swallowed hard. My voice trembled. "Then I'm asking a favor. Of you. Please."

His eyebrow arched. "Well…now, that is tempting." He turned to face me fully and stepped toward me.

Heart racing, I backed up. "So can you do it?" My breaths quickened. "Can you get us permission to be on the island without risk?"

"That's not a favor within my power to grant. The king has never granted anyone such a favor since he was imprisoned in the North Sea. It's a matter of principle. Or spite."

"Is the King of the North Sea so immune to pleas for mercy that he won't even consider granting my mother's request? I swear we mean no harm."

Scoffing, he set his hands on his narrow waist. He took another step closer. "And why should any of you be shown mercy? You deserve nothing."

"That's rather the point of mercy." I bumped into the wall. "If we deserved it, it wouldn't be mercy."

His lips trembled in the barest hint of a true smile. He stopped in front of me and pressed his hand against the wall near my head, caging me in as he leaned closer. He was so close, I could smell him. Salty ambergris, white patchouli, and spiced rum overwhelmed my senses.

I blinked, struggling to steady myself as his bright-green eyes homed in on mine. My pulse raged.

"Of course," he murmured, his voice low and silky. "My offer still stands."

I pressed myself back against the wall, palms against the coarse wood. "What offer?"

"To come to my home. My lair, as you called it." His gaze raked over me, leaving me breathless. That smile curled at his lips as his eyes grew sharper, hungrier. The claws on the hand pressed against the wall tapped against the wood.

"You just threatened everyone on this ship, and you think I would agree to run off with you?" I forced the words out. But I was wondering what would happen if I said yes.

His smirk wavered. Then he leaned closer, his breath wisping over my cheek. "Except you're thinking about it." His eyebrow lifted.

"No!" I snapped. Or at least I tried. The word came out so much weaker and softer. There was something about him. Something in the way he looked at me that stole my breath and my strength. I swallowed hard. "I'm not tempted at all." My voice cracked.

He smirked.

"Maybe I was a little before you threatened this ship," I said, stumbling over my words. "But I don't associate with people who kill for no reason."

"It isn't without reason," he murmured. His eyes had grown harder.

"The answer is still no."

He slid his left hand against my throat, pushing me harder against the wall.

Heat spasmed through me.

His body did not press against mine though his other arm kept me caged. The tips of his claws pressed against my skin, making my flesh prickle and tingle. He caressed the column of my throat with the blade of his thumb. "Is it really?" His eyes half shaded as he leaned closer to me, his mouth a whisper's breadth from my ear. "What could I offer you to make you say yes, clever girl? I can't grant you permission to be in the North Sea or protection on the island. But something else..."

My mouth went dry. *Think.* I had to think of something clever or witty to say.

But as my lips parted, he moved away from my ear and back in front of my face, his nose so close it nearly brushed mine. That spicy, heady scent made me want to collapse against him and just breathe him in. "All I want is my sister back. I know that might not be possible, so I'll take Mama and me finding some life beyond this madness. That's all."

"Hmmm. Is it really?" His gaze narrowed. He didn't move away. "You humans are so fragile. You don't even need someone to ensure your kind don't survive. Why would anyone forbid your presence? Nature would destroy you in less time than it would take to blink."

"One would think you wouldn't worry about enforcing such laws against us then." I forced my voice to remain steady. Why was this so hard? Was it some sort of glamour coming off him? It couldn't be. Shifter fae didn't have glamour.

I dropped my gaze. Something about his eyes made me feel like I was sinking and being drawn in all at once. Like I was bound to him. Somehow. "We're harmless. I swear it. We're just looking for my sister. It won't hurt anyone to let us go there."

"Just laws apply to all, darling. Weak and strong alike. I could snap your neck and spine as easily as I could puncture your flesh with my claws. And yet…yet there is both fire and iron in your eyes. You've seen things on your journey, haven't you? And you accused me of killing without reason. An unusual distinction. Most would have accused me simply of killing. Have you killed someone for good reason, clever girl?"

My heart lurched. "What difference does it make?"

His smile broadened. "Tell me the truth. I can't help but notice no one's followed you. And no one noticed you were missing during that ordeal the other day. It's almost as if you don't exist. Do you think your mother would be upset to see you here with me? Or do you think maybe she was hoping you'd come here and offer yourself? It seems like she is so caught up in how to save her youngest she's willing to sacrifice her eldest. Not that it's uncommon for parents to make such decisions when their little ones' lives are at stake. We all have to make hard choices." He drummed his claws against the wood of the wall behind my head. "You have hard choices ahead of you as well. Especially if this ship remains on the course we all know it is."

Anger flared within me. I bit it back and forced the words out. "Captain Hosvir was clear about our destination, our route, and our intentions. We are not lawbreakers."

"And your mother is set on reaching this oracle as soon as possible, second only to getting to that island. The North Sea boundary is always shifting, and the island falls right within that point. Trust me, I've been here long enough to know what happens next." He stroked a line down my throat with his claw. "And a clever girl like you knows it too, Mena." He whispered my name, his hot breath tickling my neck. "You'd be so much better off with me."

I hated the smug way he looked at me, but it took all my strength not to shiver at his voice or arch against his touch.

47

My fingers curled against my palms, heat flaring through me. I hated him. "Never."

"So you say, but who knows what the coming days may bring, darling?" He tapped his finger against my lower lip. He then glanced down the corridor. "Really, I must admit, after how this has all played out, I'm starting to wonder if anyone here would even notice if I scooped you up and carried you off. If I could get them permission to be safely on the island, they'd probably *give* you to me. Just offer you up like a sacrificial lamb. Trade the daughter they have for the one they want—"

I struck him across the face.

THE BOUNDARY

*T*hat had been a mistake.

My cheeks burned. Fear flared through me, almost enough to counter my rage. But I didn't drop my gaze. Not even for a moment.

His face barely moved in response to the slap. He cut his eyes to mine, then pressed me against the wall, hand still against my throat but not too hard.

I couldn't breathe.

Couldn't move.

His gaze held mine, his face like marble.

Something flashed in his eyes. Something I couldn't read.

Then he released me, stepped back, and strode away, his expression still unreadable.

I sagged against the wall, my hand flying to the base of my throat as I drew in a shuddering breath.

The wind howled, and the ship rocked.

Salt's bane, that man's scent and his body so close to mine warred with my anger at his words and his refusal to help.

It didn't matter though.

JESSICA M. BUTLER

I steadied myself against the wall, straightened, and then hurried back to the study.

Mama was still sobbing, shaking so badly she couldn't even stand. Captain Hosvir remained at her side. He'd moved them both to a bench fastened to the wall in between the shelves, and he just held her, his gaze focused wholly on her.

It was hard to see Mama looking so broken. Harder still knowing I had nothing to offer for comfort. Not even my presence really.

I crossed over and knelt beside her. "I couldn't fix it. I'm sorry."

Mama gripped my hand and continued to sob as if she had been shattered.

"Don't blame yourself," Hosvir said, giving me a surprisingly soft look for his fearsome appearance. That gentleness was often present when he dealt with Mama. His brow remained furrowed, the wrinkles deep along his forehead and crinkling around his eyes. "The King of the North Sea is colder than these waters. He uses the blood of his enforcers and servants to bolster his magic and controls their very lives. They've given him everything, yet he thinks nothing of them. There was no chance he'd give mercy for those he thinks of even less. He's a cruel and vengeful ruler. It was a long shot."

"What's so important about this island that we can risk certain death? Those grounded staircases and portals are—" I stopped short when I saw the bowl of stew I'd brought Mama on the floor. Based on the amount, Mama had eaten next to nothing.

I bit back a frustrated sigh and moved to clean it up.

"Your ma found some records and lore 'bout them staircases into the air. Some are fixed, and some are open. Ancient magic. Not fae or anything we know from here. Maybe not even entirely of this world. But they contain

48

secrets and may grant wishes." He shrugged. "She's been figuring out how to use them more reliably. This is the closest one. The next closest is a couple miles beyond the boundary and at the bottom of the shallows."

It still didn't make much sense to me. Everyone knew how dangerous unknown magic and staircase portals were. But over the years, Mama's willingness to explore dangerous options had intensified.

I stayed with Mama a bit longer before helping her to her cabin with Hosvir's help, ensuring she had everything she needed.

Then I went to my own bed and listened to her cry herself to sleep. Usually I dreamed of the fights and arguments, an endless cycle of accomplishing nothing but hurt feelings and wounded hearts.

This night though, once I fell asleep, I dreamed of Corvin: his bright-green eyes, his hands, his intensity, and his words. I replayed the moment I slapped him over and over again in my mind.

Next morning, I rose, expecting to find that we were headed back toward the Salt Channel and abandoning the island because of the boundary issue. Instead, I found that almost everyone was preparing to leave. Apparently they were going to risk the boundary line shifting. Mama had to see the island and test her theory.

I stayed aboard the ship. Going onto the island when it was that close to a shifting boundary line was foolish. I had as much hope of the island actually holding the secret to finding Erryn as I did of my words making a difference.

Mama stood next to one of the smaller boats that was being prepared for the journey over.

"I don't understand this." I crossed over, holding my tattered shawl close as the wind tugged at it. "Even if takes a couple months more to reach the Oracle of the Glass Mountains, at least we'll make it. There's nothing on that island that's worth risking death!"

"There are staircases that lead into the air. They are dangerous most of the time, but sometimes they can be strengthened and lead to specific portals that may go to magical places. The one on this island probably won't work as well, but it will contain more knowledge that we may be able to use," Mama said. "We may even be able to strengthen it and use it to learn more. It may give us the key to finding your sister."

"It sounds like nonsense to me," I said, sharper than I intended. I hugged myself tight. "This is ridiculous. I can't believe the captain's letting you do this!"

Mama shook her head, clicking her tongue. The sharpness had returned to her gaze, her manner more steely rather than weepy. "Saving your sister is not nonsense."

A low growl of frustration rose in me before I bit it back. There was no reasoning with her. This was pointless.

I tilted my head back. Heavy clouds rolled across the eastern sky. The sea rocked the ship, making my stomach sour. Pointless or not, I had to try. "Please. Don't go, Mama. Something bad is going to happen. We'll find Erryn, but this isn't the way."

"We're two miles out from the boundary line," Captain Hosvir said, his tone gruff and his features drawn into a scowl. "And we didn't come all this way for nothing."

Was he only doing this for Mama or was there something else? No one else was raising concerns. Already three of the longboats had been outfitted and prepared to head out.

"We'll stock up on supplies. Replenish the water stores. Forage what we can. Ophelia can do her tasks." Captain Hosvir gave a firm nod as if that settled everything. Then he returned his attention to Mama.

I bit the inside of my lip. We weren't that low on water or

food. We could turn around and sail for another ten days and reach another port.

But I wasn't the one giving orders.

I might as well not even talk.

Almost three quarters of the crew and all of the hunting otters went to the island.

Captain Hosvir invited me again. But I refused and just watched until Mama got into the longboat and reached the shore. Mama refused to look at me. Not even to wave. Maybe she was lost in thought, or maybe she genuinely didn't see. But really...no—Mama was mad at me again.

We were probably going to have another big fight when she got back.

Especially when she realized—again—that this wasn't the solution to finding Erryn.

Disappointment and hopelessness brought out the worst in both of us.

I wandered through the ship. When I reached the study, I found Mama's book. She must have forgotten it. It looked like it had fallen out of her bag.

This she would miss.

I picked it up and flipped through it. It was all about the ancient magics and staircases in the air and other strange phenomenon. She'd probably come back for it.

Picking the book up, I returned to the stern of the ship, gazing out at the island shrouded in fog and mist. As I waited, I read.

The words didn't stick in my mind. I had to read and reread. My focus kept returning to the water and the island. The island, from this distance, looked ordinary. A sandy beach with grey stones and a coniferous forest farther back. The fog did not dissolve as the watery-yellow sun rose higher in the sky.

A storm was coming.

That pressure in my stomach and up through my chest coiled and expanded.

I wanted to throw up.

Hurry back, Mama.

I tugged at my hair as I glanced around.

Numerous white stone pillars and jagged spires jutted up from the sea like bones. These were narrower than the ones I'd used to get back to the ship, and they rose much higher above the waves. Some even looked to have pocket caves and indentations large enough for a person to stand on. If ever people had lived in this place before the wars, people had likely fished in those places.

Now the strange rocks reminded me of death. The clouds darkened, taking over more than half the sky. The rumbling of thunder intensified.

Movement at the beach caught my eye.

Relief poured through me. Yes! They were getting in the longboats. I spotted Mama in her green shawl.

They were on their way back.

I watched as they made their preparations, everyone moving swiftly and with purpose.

A strange scent reached me, bitter and acrid, like lightning and venom.

Something moved in the water, coming up from the bottom and floating into sight.

I halted.

No.

Not one something.

Strange shapes moved in the water. Large and pale, somewhere between lavender and pink. They wriggled and spasmed.

Jellyfish?

The sentry in the crow's nest shouted. "Boundary line's moving! Boundary line's moving!"

My gaze snapped up. The three longboats in the water still had a ways to go. Jellyfish were swarming around them as well. A great column of them. The boundary was made of jellyfish?

The wind howled as it strengthened, and the sea roughened.

I tucked the book into my dress pocket and prepared to help.

Something scraped against the side of the ship.

I spun as the rain spattered against my face, cold and sharp as needles.

Thunder cracked and lightning flashed, highlighting the figure that now stood on the tentacled carving at the end of the stern.

Corvin!

A DESPERATE BARGAIN

*C*orvin's cloak billowed and whipped against him, his silhouette dark against the greying sky. "This ship will be destroyed," he said, his voice cold as the rain grew stronger and the wind sliced against the ship. "The warnings were given in due time. Your captain did not listen."

My blood thundered in my ears. "It's the storms," I protested, hugging the charcoal wool shawl around my shoulders. "They're on their way back." There was no denying that they were beyond the boundary. "As soon as they're back, we'll leave."

"The law has no mercy, and I have no choice." His voice remained hard, but a twinge of something—sorrow, disappointment, anger, grief?—passed through his eyes. "The ship must be destroyed."

"Please." I crossed closer to the railing as I looked up at him. My heart raced faster, my tongue thick in my mouth. I almost reached out to grip his trouser leg and then fell back, holding my hands to my chest. "There has to be something you can do. Otherwise, you wouldn't be here. There's a reason you're telling me this."

Thunder boomed, and the ship heaved on the swelling waves. I lurched forward and grabbed the railing. Somehow he remained steady, simply moving with the ship as if he were a part of it.

"I don't want you to die," he said roughly. His eyes narrowed on me as he crouched down. Leaning forward, his hand rose to my cheek, his claws grazing my skin.

My breath caught in my throat. I struggled to process his words as the wind tore at my hair and shawl. "If you destroy this ship, I will die."

"Not if you come with me." His gaze hooded, his voice going lower and becoming more urgent. "I can protect you. I will protect you. Just come with me."

"And leave everyone else?" I set my jaw, resisting the urge to look back toward the island and the boats that were desperately struggling through the mounting waves and the torrents of jellyfish.

"I don't care about them," he said, his voice darkening. "I care about you." He reached for my wrist.

I shook my head, drawing back, hand clasping my shawl. "What about a bargain? You fae love bargains, right?" My skin crawled even as I said it, but it was all I could think of.

He raised an eyebrow. "What are you offering?" The low music of his voice intensified. "You'll come with me willingly?"

"I'll come with you to your home so long as you swear to spare every living being from this crew." My voice shook at the end, but I steadied it, my gaze fixed on him.

He paused, mulling things over. The muscles in his jaw and neck tightened. "I cannot spare the ship, but I can see to it that all who were upon it survive. If you come with me." He said the last part low and husky, the words vibrating through my core.

Terror chilled me more than the rain. I forced myself to

meet his gaze. "Then I accept your bargain. I swear that I will come with you to your home if you swear to ensure that all from this ship survive."

That sharp hunger returned to his eyes. He reached out to take hold of me, but I held up my hands. "No. You have to show me that you spared everyone."

He grunted, his eyes narrowing. "And how am I to accomplish that?"

"Get creative," I said sharply. "But the bargain requires that everyone survives." I had to at least see that Mama lived. A greasy ball of emotion formed in my stomach, sickening me. "Swear to me."

He scoffed, then set his hands on his broad black belt. For a breath, he seemed to consider this. He nodded. "I swear it." He breathed those words with the solemness of a vow. "But you cannot remain on the ship. I'll put you somewhere you can see what is happening and where you'll be safe. The ship will break apart soon. We cannot delay."

Though part of me wanted to argue, the other part recognized he was speaking the truth. I nodded.

Just like that, he put his arm around my waist and whisked me into his arms. The waves thundered and roared almost as much as the heavens. Rain lashed at my face, stinging like needles even when I turned away. My stomach lurched with the ship as it pitched and swayed.

How was he staying steady?

The few sailors who'd remained behind struggled to man their various posts, staggering and clutching at the holds and grips, ropes tied about their waists. Did they have any idea what was coming?

Almost before I realized what was happening, Corvin leaped into the air. My stomach dropped.

I flailed and clutched at him, my feet kicking in the dark air. The white-capped waves peeked and struck at the vessel, the massive column of jellyfish spreading and grasping in the waters below.

With a jarring thud, we landed on one of the stone pillars.

He dragged me beneath the overhang. "Stay here. Watch. Don't step out from underneath the shelter," he shouted in my ear. He pressed me back firmly against the pockmarked stone, both hands on my shoulders. His eyes caught the flashes of the lightning, glowing green.

I stared at him, suddenly terrified. This was the fae I'd just bargained with to save Mama and the rest of the crew. He could kill me if he chose, and there was nothing I could do to stop him.

He gave me a grim smirk, then lunged off the stone pillar.

Shivering, I clutched my soaking shawl around my shoulders. The chill sliced right through me. Already my fingers and toes burned from the cold.

Lightning lit up the sky in forked branches and multi-tongued formations. It froze the scene for the briefest of breaths, then faded into darkness. The ship fought against the waves.

I edged farther out to search for the three boats in the water.

There!

Lightning flashed again, illuminating the terrified faces of the passengers huddled together. The dwarves rowed with all their might against the crashing waves.

My eyes searched frantically for Mama. Where was she? Another bolt lit up the water—there—in the rearmost boat! Mama's ashen face stood out among the others, locked in fear as she clung to the side, her hair and green shawl plastered against her.

Where had Corvin gone?

Lightning struck again. Now there were dark shapes in the waters. Two massive crocodilian creatures swam beneath the ship, the pale, pulsing jellyfish parting to allow them passage. The sky darkened with billowing thunderheads dominating the horizon.

The longboat with Mama tipped up.

I jammed my hand against my mouth. "Mama!" I screamed. The wind ripped my voice into the howling void.

A dark shape moved beneath the boat as the wave crested.

My breath locked in my throat.

I couldn't tear my gaze from Mama's panic-stricken face. Everything condensed to that single moment. My heart thundered in my ears as I watched helplessly. Bile filled my throat, my lips and face stinging from the sharp salt water striking me.

A yellow-and-green striped form snapped up around the boat as the wave crashed over. The passengers emerged, choking and gagging. A jellyfish straggled across the side. One of the sailors flipped it over the edge with an oar.

I dug my fingers into my cheek as I kept my hand over my mouth, staring, transfixed.

It was all right. A ragged breath trembled through me.

Mama was alive. He'd gotten to her in time. She was going to be all right.

When lightning flared across the sky once more, I saw that Corvin had retrieved the second boat as well and dragged both up onto the beach in his massive coils.

He bellowed something. Probably for them to stay. Then he lunged back into the water, his enormous body sliding beneath the choppy waves.

I cast my gaze over the sea for the rest of the sailors and the ship. The third boat had capsized. Four of the ten clung to the sides. One had already righted the longboat, gotten back in, and now fought to drag the others up. The others splashed and flailed in the water, shouting. Red whip-like lashes cut across their arms, and jellyfish stings tore over their trousers.

Corvin swept in.

The jellyfish immediately pulsed away from him, repelled. He wrapped around the boat, gathering up each of the survivors and depositing them in the vessel with devastatingly swift ease.

I hugged myself tight as I watched, shivering and chilling. With every passing minute, the storm worsened.

The noise deafened me.

A powerful gust nearly sent me staggering forward. Wincing, I forced myself back deeper into the stone nook.

The *Seaforger's Pride* struggled against the fury of the storm. The waves cracked and slammed against it with punishing force.

In another flash of lightning, I glimpsed Corvin leaping onto the main deck. He moved across the ship unaffected by the water and cold. As if he existed outside it, somehow. Perhaps it was fae magic or experience or both.

As soon as the rest of the sailors were in the last boat, some clutching bags and crates, Corvin wrapped around the longboat and dragged them through the raging sea to the beach.

My heart leaped as I glimpsed the beach. Mama was only a distant figure, standing out because of her moss-green shawl. I could see her ashen face when I closed my eyes. Hosvir would look after her, wouldn't he? She'd be all right. She was alive. That's what mattered.

The lion-sized hunting otters bounded around the dwarves as well, tugging at their sleeves and coats to pull them back from the beach and the lashing waves.

A loud, abrupt crack resounded through the air.

My attention snapped back to the ship.

Corvin circled it now, a great wound in the ship's side as if he had punched through it. As large as his eel form had been before, he became even larger now. Long enough to wrap around the entirety of the caravel. He struck at it again.

The dark reptilian forms below surged up. One seized the tentacled carving at the stern while the other seized the figurehead. The ship bowed and bent for one dreadful moment, then snapped like kindling. Corvin pummeled it. He lashed at the masts and shredded the furled sails as the monstrous reptiles around him rent through the wood like paper.

My breath snagged in my throat.

No one could have survived that.

This was the fulfillment of the fae law of the sea.

This was the plan.

The plan if I had not made my bargain.

The cold cut and spiraled deeper within me. Nausea twisted in my stomach. Clutching the soaking shawl tighter about my shoulders, I struggled to comprehend it all. The carnage that might have existed here. That did exist when people crossed the boundary.

A sturdy *thud* struck the rock near me.

I looked up. Every muscle in my body tightened, a heaviness crushing down upon me.

Corvin stood at the edge of the spire, drenched. "It's done. Thirty-five passengers. Twelve hunting otters. They're all safe on the shore. So long as they do not enter the waters, they will be safe."

I stared past him into the darkness at the island where Mama mourned. There were a thousand things I wanted to tell her now. None of them the harsh words that had sprung to mind countless times over the past years. Only comfort.

And now that the moment to go with Corvin was here, all

I felt was fear. Fear for a thousand different things. To suddenly know that this distant, bleary look might be the last time I saw Mama and that my last words to her were to tell her were harsh. "Did you tell her I'm safe?"

Lightning flared again. His bright-green eyes widened, then he laughed in bewilderment and shrugged. " Let her make her own inferences. There wasn't exactly time for a proper conversation."

I opened my mouth to protest, but he shushed me. "I fulfilled my part of the bargain. Now keep yours."

Anger and hate flared through me. I wanted to strike him. But a bargain was a bargain. At least Mama and everyone else was alive. There wasn't anything else left. I had to keep my word.

I gave a sharp nod. "Fine!"

"Put your arms around my neck," he said.

I complied. His arms encircled me, bringing me tight against his chest. Already his heat reached me, even more intense for the cold water that pounded down around us. His hair was slicked down, trails of rain and salt water running down his face and neck. Yet his heart thudded with a startlingly steady rhythm. He swept one arm beneath me and lifted me up against his chest like a bride to be carried over the threshold.

I found myself curling against him simply for the warmth, and I hated myself for it.

Another flash of lightning illuminated him. His face had a grim cast to it as he studied me, his thumb pressed to my lower lip. "This next part is going to be uncomfortable. Deep breath, clever girl."

I barely had time to comply before he leaped off the edge of the jagged stone spire, out of the safety of the cave, and into the seething waters below.

NOT A FAE PALACE

The freezing temperature drove the breath from my lungs as soon as we plunged under.

I clung to him now, clinging to him despite my pride. Even though I squeezed my eyelids shut, the saltwater stung my eyes and filled my nostrils and mouth.

Corvin held me fast. He swam a short ways before we emerged beneath a rocky overhang where the waters were not so rough and the rain did not reach us. Thunder cracked, and lightning flared again. "Easy there," he said, wiping the water from my face.

I coughed and spluttered as I gulped in a deep breath of fresh air. "This is it?" It was so cold. I just wanted to get out of the water.

He shook his head. "Sorry, darling. Just taking a breather. Seas are rough during storms, and you can't make it to my home on one breath."

My teeth chattered. "How far?"

"Nothing for you to worry about. Just take more deep breaths. I promise I won't let you drown. You did well." His hand brushed my hair back behind my ears, his voice more concerned than stern now. "But this is the really hard part, all right?"

I barely had time to nod and take another deep gulp of air before he pulled me tight against his chest and dove down once more.

The cold stabbed into my skin. All thoughts of dignity faded as I held onto him. The powerful currents tugged around me. He seemed to navigate them with ease, sliding and ducking and moving along some course I couldn't see. Each time we resurfaced, the storm had lessened. And at last, he dove straight down with me in his arms.

Down we went.

Down.

Down.

The pressure intensified, my ears popping and my head spinning. The rushing gargle and roar of it all filled me.

It stung my eyes too much to dare more than a tiny, blurry glimpse into the darkness of the sea.

There was nothing.

My lungs burned, aching and near to bursting. I clutched at his shoulder, wriggling. He knew I needed air. He'd taken me up to breathe before. Had he forgotten?

Please.

Air.

I needed air!

Then—just when I felt I couldn't take it anymore—Corvin propelled us upward, and we emerged.

With a gasp and sputter, I started choking in as much air I could manage. Half were full of seawater, making me gag. My throat and nose burned, the water streaking through my eyes. It was dark here. And cold.

Oh, I hated the cold.

Corvin pressed the hair back from my face as I hacked. "Almost there." He looked concerned as he studied me.

There were a thousand things I wanted to say to him. Complaints, pleas, observations. All I could get out was the coughing.

The horrid, horrid coughing as I struggled to get a clear breath. My stomach clenched and cramped.

"Easy there. Just breathe, clever girl." He lifted me out of the water and set me on my feet.

My knees gave way. I lurched forward, throwing up salt and bile.

Pale-blue light flared, revealing a dark-walled cave.

Through tear-streaked eyes, I struggled to take in my surroundings.

First thing was his expression: his creased forehead, arched eyebrows, and pinched mouth.

This wasn't going the way he'd expected.

He crouched beside me, a pale-blue orb in his hand, his claws curled around it. The orb cast eerie, claw-like shadows across the wall. "Let's get you inside. Can you walk?"

I wiped my mouth with the back of my hand. More coughs shuddered through my body. Glaring at him blearily, I pushed myself up. "I can."

I cast my gaze around the cave, noting that while the cave itself was small, there was a large, heavy door with dull iron bands set into the wall a little behind us.

He moved to help me stand, but I pushed him away with a ragged huff. "I don't need your help." The words rasped from my throat before I succumbed to another shaking cough.

Somehow he was already dry, his hair once more full and soft, while I was fairly certain I looked like a wrung out, half-drowned rat.

His eyebrow lifted more. It seemed he had not expected my refusal. But he crossed to the door. With one claw, he traced a symbol on the metal of the band. It glowed bright yellow, then the door creaked open.

He glanced back at me, his expression now masked and hard. Then he strode through the door, expecting me to follow.

Part of me wanted to tell him that I'd fulfilled my part of the bargain now. I'd come to his home.

But I wasn't in any condition to run. And I had no idea how to escape yet. That swim would kill me if I tried it on my own.

The water was black as ink and still as a mirror. I hugged myself as the seawater dripped from my hair and clothes, forming puddles across the stone. Even breathing hurt.

He waited for me beyond the doorway with a small waterskin. "Here. Drink this."

"What is it?" I asked, my voice cracking.

"A kind of tonic and water. For the throat."

I was a little surprised that he had that, but I accepted it and took a long drink. The bitter flavor flooded my mouth, but the relief was almost immediate. I drank deeply, muscles aching.

As I did, he circled out into the room and started lighting additional pale-blue orbs by tapping his orb to each one. The chamber had been outfitted with the scraps of numerous wrecks. Shelves and shelves of random items as well as scrapped bits of furniture made it seem like a chaotic store-room that someone was living in. Very little was present in the way of fabrics. All of the wood was water-stained. The books that were present had all been soaked and dried, leading to their bindings being ragged and bulging with crinkled pages that had never returned to their former smoothness. These were spread out on the shelves, despite his saying that he couldn't read.

Glass bottles hung suspended from the ceiling by strings. Blue fungi or gel or something oozy-looking filled the bottoms, and faint light glowed from each one, most pale blue but a few pale lavender. Droplets of salt water wept down some of the sleek, dark walls, pooling in the creases of the cracked stone floor.

It was depressing. Not at all what I had expected.

Three different doors had been fastened into the wall. Two did not appear to be well set. The third had similar bands to the one we had entered through, suggesting that perhaps it was an exit.

I managed another sip of the tonic and grimaced.

The air was damp and cold. I shivered, the water still dripping off me.

I was going to die down here. That was all there was to it. Mama wouldn't know how much I loved her. And how much I regretted being so harsh. I should have given her a hug, even if she was mad at me. I should have told her I loved her again. I'd told her thousands of times, and I wanted to tell her a thousand more.

The knot of emotion in my throat choked me.

My mood soured as I hugged myself.

"You're cold?" He tilted his head.

The way he looked at me no longer charmed me at all.

I glared at him. "Of course I'm cold, you thick-skulled shifter. You dragged me down under the ocean in the middle of a storm! I don't even have a coat." I bit back the tears that rose to my eyes. And right now all I really wanted was to hug Mama and make sure she was all right.

"If you'd had a coat, it would be wet as well. Like your shawl and everything else." The orb still cradled in his palm, he strode toward a dark portion of the room and tapped it to another glistening crystal orb. It lit up, revealing a large wardrobe. He set his orb in a black iron ring and opened the wardrobe, releasing a musty scent rich with incense, cedar, and lavender. He leaned inside and pulled out a few garments. "Here. You can change. Something should fit."

I accepted the armload of clothes, trying to make sense of this place. Was it a storage room? "Do you not have a fire down here?"

There was no heat source that I could see. Really no furniture for comfort unless you counted the thin rush mats that sat on the floor and some crooked stools and chairs. The shelves with knickknacks and cupboards looked as if they had been ripped out of multiple ships and haphazardly dominated most of the walls. A large table leaned crooked on three legs with a stack of books serving as the fourth. No hearth or fireplace or stove. Not even a fire ring. "Nothing at all for heat?"

"No." He raised an eyebrow at me. He indicated the door behind me. "You can change in there. It's where you'll stay."

The door practically sagged open when I pressed my hand to it. Inside was a broken end table, a half pitcher, cracked mirror, and a thin, discolored mat that might have started to mold. A thin blanket had been folded up at the foot.

My shoulders dropped.

Corvin closed the wardrobe and opened the door next to it, revealing another room.

My eyes widened. "Is that your bedroom?" I asked, indicating it with a flip of my hand.

That room was almost as sparse as the guest room. A thin, ragged blanket lay mounded at the foot of the mat. Something like a coat or a dress had been balled up to form a circle. Tagger lay on that, tail pressed up over his little snout. A wooden chair sat in the corner with a sagging dresser next to it. The lowest drawer had edged out.

He nodded, his head tilted as he studied me. "Yes…"

"This is your home…not just some outpost you stay in?" I couldn't believe this place. Was that fungus growing on the wall?

"This is where I live," he said, his voice tighter.

"How could anyone live like this? This isn't fit for living. Not even for animals." It just slipped out.

He flinched. His expression twisted into a scowl as he opened his mouth to speak.

THE ESCAPE

As soon as I said that, I knew it was a mistake. It sounded so much harsher than I intended, and—even though I was angry at having to leave Mama behind and this whole bargain—I immediately regretted it.

Easy as the words were to speak, they were impossible to take back and almost as impossible to counter.

Corvin closed his mouth, his expression hard as the stone the cave was carved from. Then he turned, walked into his room, and slammed the door. The door creaked and snapped into place, grating against the stone.

Guilt flared through me. I ducked my chin, more tears welling up. That had come out wrong.

Still trembling from the cold, I hugged the musty garments to my chest. I drew in a deep breath. The lavender reminded me of Mama back before we spent everything searching for Erryn.

It was too much.

I burst into tears.

For all the good it did, I just sobbed.

On top of all that, it was so hard to get warm. My fingers

and toes ached and burned. Stripping off my still-wet socks and shoes made them sting even more. And the cold damp in the air made it worse. Even wrapping up in the old robe did little to curb the cold.

I piled the extra garments up as well as the blanket and curled up on the mat. It was so thin I could feel every pit and dent in the stone floor beneath it.

Everyone was alive though. This hadn't been a mistake. It was the only choice.

I told myself that over and over until I cried myself to sleep.

I woke, shivering. How much longer before I got deathly ill?

Probably not much.

It was no wonder parents warned their children against bargains with fae if they wound up in places like this.

Shuddering, I sat up and limped out to the main room, rubbing my arms as I went.

Corvin was nowhere to be seen. Neither was Tagger.

"Hello?" I called out softly. "Hello?" I spoke louder this time. "I'm sorry about what I said. I didn't mean for it to sound so bad." My cheeks and chest stung with shame. It was clear that my words had struck a deep chord in him. Almost as if he were embarrassed.

As I rubbed my arms and stomped my feet to get the blood flowing, I continued to search.

No sign of him anywhere.

If I was going to find a way out, now was the time to do it.

Not by water. That wasn't the way out. But there might be another way.

I searched around the common room. There was a plate sitting out on the table with strips of salted, dried fish on it. A piece of wrinkled paper sat next to it with a picture of a stick person with a skirt putting something in her mouth and an arrow pointing at the fish. I frowned a little. A large blue pitcher with a superficial crack down its side sat beyond that with a similar picture of a stick woman drinking from it.

That was thoughtful. But I was his prisoner. If he wanted me to survive, he had to feed me. This didn't mean anything.

I had to figure out something fast.

My stomach cramped as I imagined Mama wandering the beach.

How long before Mama accepted I was dead and gone, and went back to searching for Erryn? And how was Mama going to get off the beach? They'd probably send up a smoke signal or something. But that could take a few days.

Creator, let Hosvir care for Mama.

I pressed my lips in a tight line, my appetite fading.

Despite the nausea and discomfort, I forced myself to eat the dried, salted fish and drink the water. I hadn't eaten since yesterday, and commonsense encouraged eating when I could. Even if it did taste foul and fishy.

It left an oily residue on the inside of my mouth. I'd experimented with a number of salting and drying techniques in my journeys over the past years. Some methods worked better than others, but this one created a foul aftertaste that coated my tongue.

Still, it filled my belly, and it gave me strength.

The clothes I had hung up to dry overnight were still damp. The oversized robe, trousers, and tunic would have to do. I couldn't go without socks and shoes though. I found a spare pair of oversized socks to wear, but my shoes were still damp and I had no alternative.

I cringed, knowing if I wasn't careful I'd have blisters and sores on my feet before the day was over. But if I was going to escape, I couldn't do it barefoot.

Ugh.

It was horrid.

I'd had to deal with wet feet so much over the years, and it never got any easier. I retrieved my clip from my dress. It still held my wooden spoon. I then grabbed a spare sock with a hole in it and found a knife in the main room. Better than nothing, at least.

I then checked out the remaining doors. One was firmly locked, but it didn't seem to have runes on it. The other was set the most firmly into the wall and locked securely. It was also directly across from the water entrance, and if my knowledge of runes was correct, it said something like "cave exists here."

I pried and picked at it for a while before concluding that the entire locking and security mechanism was based on the runes in addition to a heavy deadbolt.

Being on a ship run by dwarves meant I'd seen a number of runes used for various tasks, but that didn't mean I knew how to work them. However, Mik and Hosvir both had shown me an effective way to handle runic locks: break the area around it and apply leverage from the weakest point of the lock, which, thankfully, was on the inside.

I picked up a heavy stone from the floor and started hammering at the door. The solid *thwacks* resounded through the chamber. Bits of stone chipped away, falling to the floor. After a few minutes of pounding, small fissures had developed, spreading out from around the lock like spiderwebs. I then rummaged around in the cupboards until I found what I needed: a crowbar.

For what felt like hours, I chipped and pried away at the door until the lock snapped and the door cracked open.

A waft of sharp air greeted me.

Swallowing hard, I peered out into the dark passage beyond. There was a fresh, bracing draft coming from somewhere, even if it did smell heavily of salt and algae. That was a good sign. Right? Who knew how far away it was? But something was better than nothing.

A small tremor passed through me. Almost a sensation of guilt. What was that about?

I put my hand to my chest, wincing.

If I didn't know better, it felt like…deep down, something told me not to leave Corvin. Not just something. Like deep down, I didn't want to leave him.

But why?

He was the reason our ship had been destroyed. Even if it was on the king's orders, he had followed those orders. There had been no harm done by our visiting the island. Especially not when the boundary's movement was so arbitrary.

This was strange.

It was almost as if a thread bound me to him. A thread that thrummed with disapproval for the briefest of moments, sending a pang of regret through my core. Warning me that leaving him would take away something precious.

And unlike other encounters I'd had with fae magic, it felt…clear. Pure, even.

Shaking my head, I tried to take in what this meant. That thrumming vibration passed as I focused on it. Almost as if it was too tenuous to exist.

And all I was left with was an awareness of the darkness.

It was so horribly dark and cold down here.

Why did he live down here like this? How could he live like this?

I picked up two orbs. One I deposited in the oversized pocket of the long charcoal robe. The second I gripped in one hand while holding the crowbar in the other.

Time to do this.

With a deep breath, I stepped out into the dark passage. The pale-blue orb cast a small circle of light around me, and my steps echoed in the cavernous expanse. It was even colder out here, but all my hammering and pounding at the door had at least gotten blood flowing again. Even if my feet were disgustingly damp.

I studied this area. My sense of direction was usually fairly decent. But there were five passages that I could see. It was unlikely any were a straight shot up.

Another twinge passed through me. No. I refused to listen to that. I'd kept my word. I'd fulfilled the bargain and come down here to his home. It was perfectly fine for me to escape now. Why would I owe him anything?

His face flashed back into my mind. His expression the last time we'd spoken.

I cringed inwardly as I recalled how he had flinched at my words. Shaking my head, I tried to brush it off. Why did I feel so bad about that? I owed him nothing. He'd been willing to let everyone on the ship die. And he'd killed others before.

I shook my head. It wasn't as if he was a friend or a family member. He was practically a stranger.

He was worse.

Basically, an enemy.

So why did some part of me want to stay close to him? There was actually an ache inside me that intensified like a tender bruise when I focused on it.

No!

I shook my head, trying to push the thoughts away.

I needed to focus. There were other far more important questions. Like which way to go?

The only sound was the echo of dripping water somewhere ahead. It was so dark, my eyes couldn't adjust to it.

I stepped forward, examining each of the different passages. The faint glow of the orb lit my way. Two of the paths angled upward. One smelled fresher than the other.

I unfastened a bit of thread from the ripped sock, fastened it securely around a stalagmite and started forward.

The cold air bit at my cheeks as I walked, and I tucked my free hand into a pocket for warmth. The orb cast dancing shadows against the rough stone walls as I went. The green thread that ran along behind me now was the one tether I had in case I got lost or needed to backtrack. Or, even worse, abandon my attempt to escape and return and hope Corvin didn't notice what I'd attempted... although explaining the broken stone and the twisted lock might be hard to pass off as anything other than an escape attempt.

The tunnel twisted and turned, sometimes sloping up or down but mostly moving up. Often it branched, and I had to choose.

Each time, I relied on my nose.

More than once, I had to squeeze through narrow gaps between boulders or step carefully over treacherous piles of loose stone. My shoes squelched unpleasantly with every step. The steady dripping of water remained constant.

So strange to be down here.

My heart still hammered, the shadows twitching and snagging my attention.

It wasn't my first time navigating an unknown cave, but it was the first time I'd had to start within its depths. Hosvir had told me a few things about navigating the caves in these parts, as had Mik and a few of the others. Mostly summaries of their own exploits and explorations when their vessel docked and they continued their research. But some of their tidbits helped.

I was violating a crucial one in that I didn't have two separate types of light sources and no real knowledge of how to operate these orbs. But it was better than nothing.

On I went.

I half expected Corvin to come racing after me. Every shadow reminded me of him. And then—well, who knew what he would do? Probably nothing good. He wasn't going to be happy about me running off like this.

Based on the intensity of the water pressure, I didn't think I was more than a couple hundred feet underground. If I could find a way, I'd be out of here fast. And he'd be angry.

But...I wasn't afraid of him hurting me.

I couldn't even imagine him hurting me. Not even after all I'd seen him do.

He'd probably just look at me with those bright-green eyes and...be all hurt. But that was his problem. Not mine. I had to get back and rescue Mama. And then—

Soft footsteps pattered up behind me.

I spun around in time to see a pair of glittering eyes.

I lifted the crowbar. "Stay away," I said grimly.

The fearless creature bounded into the light, rearing up on its hind legs.

"Tagger?" I lowered the orb, blinking. Where had he come from? I peered into the darkness behind him, the thread twitching with my movement.

Tagger squeaked and then let out a series of trills. He tilted his head in a manner similar to Corvin.

"Did you come here to betray me?" I asked dryly, resting the hand with the crowbar against my hip.

He chirped and dropped on all fours. His long whiskers brushed the floor as he padded closer. His purple-black eyes sparkled.

Damn it.

He was cute. I wanted to hold him.

"Forgive me if I don't let you near my weapons." I glanced back down the passage. Had he come alone?

He bounded up beside me and started rubbing against my ankles like a cat. His soft fur tickled my calves.

What was I supposed to do with him?

I sighed, then shook my head. "Fine. You can come with me if you want. I don't suppose you know the way out?"

Tagger hopped around me, nuzzled my ankle, and spun in a circle. Then he paused, stared up at me, and made no move in any direction.

"You're very helpful," I muttered. But in truth, some part of me was relieved to have company down here. Even though most people didn't notice me, I was rarely truly alone. And it wasn't until now that I realized how comforting it was to have a little friend present.

If he was a friend. I actually wasn't certain. "You better not betray me."

I turned back in my original direction, then gave the thread a little tug.

Good.

It was still attached.

I glanced at Tagger once more, then started down the path. He padded along beside me, squeaking and trilling happily.

Pale trails of silver formed downward arrows in the dark walls, indicators of trace ore and a likely sign I was roughly headed toward the surface. Just so long as I didn't wind up lost or trapped. The drip-dripping sound soon faded, replaced only by my breaths. Sometimes the freshness of the air faltered as well.

My shoes crunched on the stone. Occasionally my hand brushed the cracked, curved wall, the cold biting into my flesh. Tagger never led the way. He just circled and chittered at everything.

Always forward.

There had to be a way out.

If I could will it into being—

Pebbles tumbled down the passage, rolling past my feet along with silt.

Tagger sat up on his hindquarters, peering out from behind me, paws at his chest.

I froze.

My heartbeat thundered louder. It echoed in my mind as I strained to hear anything else.

There was something up ahead.

I steadied my hand around the pale-blue orb and lifted it slowly to broaden the path of light before me. My palm sweat around the crowbar and the sock with its dangling thread.

The pale-blue light illuminated only a small portion of the passage. The silver veins in the wall had thickened, a hopeful indicator of being even closer to the surface. No visible signs of a predator disturbed the area.

My gut clenched harder.

Didn't matter what I saw.

Something was watching me.

DOWN

I held my breath, searching the darkness before me. Nothing but jagged, glistening stone stretched ahead. The cold air tasted of salt and mold.

Tagger didn't even make a sound as he leaned out a little farther, his gaze flicking over the passage. Then he stopped.

Soft scratches on the stone drew closer. A cat-sized cave rat darted into the light from the left tunnel. It stared at us, its bald snout twitching.

Well, that was manageable. Especially if it was just one.

Wait.

Tagger hadn't moved. He was staring at a point beyond the rat. A point far deeper in the darkness.

The rat scuttled across the passage.

A massive blue claw slammed out and speared it. The poor creature barely squeaked before it was dragged into the darkness.

I fell back, eyes wide. Tagger moved with me. My knuckles whitened as I clutched the crowbar tighter.

What was that?

A grinding series of clicks followed. Then a heavy *thud thud*.

The ground vibrated. Six pairs of small eyes glittered in the light, moving independently. As it entered the ring of light, the eyes clustered together.

I blinked, struggling to process what it was.

It was...a crab?

The twelve-eyed crab stood more than eight feet in height as it crept along the passage, its spear-like legs striking the floor. As its eyes wobbled on stalks, its mandibles worked in rapid succession. The left claw was massive, similar to a fiddler crab's but with enormous spikes at the back and base. The right claw, though smaller, had numerous spines alone the back of the claw. It moved toward us sideways.

Salt's bane.

How did you fight a giant crab?

Tagger jutted his chest out and barked.

"Stay back, baby," I said, nudging him with my leg.

The otter growled at the crab. His fur puffed up and his tail went razor straight. Hackles bristled along the back of his neck.

My muscles tightened as we continued to retreat. I had to think fast.

The rocky walls and uneven ground of the cave tunnel offered little advantage. A few loose stones littered the path, and numerous stalactites and stalagmites protruded. Some were sharp like spears, but how could I use them? Was there anywhere we could hide? A boulder I could pry loose maybe? No—even if I found one, we were moving downhill now. It'd just crush us. Damn it!

The crab stalked toward us. It waved its larger claw in a fat, lazy circle. The pinchers clicked shut, sounding like heavy pruning shears.

I continued backing up, nudging Tagger along. The otter kept grumbling and barking and hissing, but he didn't seem inclined to leave me.

If I hadn't seen how fast that crab had speared and devoured the cave rat, I might have made the mistake of thinking it was slow. Right now, it was just curious.

I stooped, slipped the orb into the same hand as the hand with the crowbar, and picked up a rock. I then chucked it so that it struck the wall behind the crab.

The loud clatter and tumble caught the crab's attention. Its antennae twitched and swayed in never-ending circles.

Please go. Please.

It scuttled into the darkness.

Claws scraped, and rocks clattered as it moved back deeper into the cave.

Then silence.

My stomach soured, nerves tightening.

Tagger chirped again, softer this time. He remained alert.

Swallowing hard, I turned in a circle, glancing around for any trace of the crab. The weak, shimmering light of the pale-blue orb revealed nothing but shining stone and cracked rocks. Shadows pressed in all around, but behind me the passage narrowed until it was barely wide enough for two people to pass through side by side.

I clicked my tongue at Tagger, forgetting for a moment that he wasn't one of the hunting otters. But he glanced up at me and responded as if he recognized the command to fall back.

Smart boy.

There had to be another way to the surface.

My instincts warned me that the crab was likely to come after us again. We hadn't seen the last of it.

The walls of the passage narrowed and bulged, forming a

strange reverse bottle shape at the top. But the crab would have a tight fit getting through to me.

Then I remembered. There had been another branching passage farther back. A little narrower with a lower ceiling.

My ears strained.

Something loud clattered and collapsed like a shifting pile of rocks. I jumped back, almost losing my grip on the crowbar.

Was there a rock slide?

Tagger raced behind me.

Dust puffed into the circle of light, chalky and unpleasant. I fanned it away as I moved back. No rocks appeared before them though. The deafening roar soon ended with a few clattering notes.

"What was that?" I murmured, staring into the darkness. Was it possible that the crab had been crushed?

I swallowed hard.

No.

No, that would be too easy.

My nerves tightened.

It was still watching us, wasn't it?

Tagger tilted his head back, then sent out a loud, trilling shriek.

I sprang back toward him, half expecting him to be pierced. But the spearing blow struck where I had just been —from above.

My eyes widened.

The massive crab was on the ceiling!

How had it gotten up there?

It released its hold.

I scrambled back, dropping the sock and dragging Tagger with me as the crab dropped down, landing with a heavy thud. Its multitude of eyes swung towards us, claws snapping menacingly.

The uneven tunnel offered little room to maneuver.

Stalactites hung like daggers above and rock formations jutted out to form precious protection. The crowbar hung heavy. I swung it around and dodged behind a rock formation as the crab slashed at me with the sharper of its claws. The metal struck the claw, sending painful vibrations through me as the crab darted back. It shook its whole body in rage, making its carapace clatter. Then it lunged.

Dropping back, I ducked under a column of stone.

The crab crashed against it. Dust and silt rained down with the horrifying crunch.

I brought the crowbar around and cracked it over the crab's legs. The crab swatted and attacked, not even losing its balance when I broke one of the smaller legs.

Everything became a blur of falling dust and jabbing claws as I fought and tried to keep Tagger and me from getting killed. The pale-blue orb slipped out of my hand and rolled into one of the crevices. I tried to grab the second out of my pocket.

It popped out of my hand.

"No!" I ducked in time to avoid the claw again. The pinchers almost seized me, nicking the edge of my skirt instead. I dropped to the ground.

Tagger continued to shriek and click. He darted in between the crab's legs.

I leaped up, grabbed one of the fallen orbs, and seized Tagger by the scuff of his neck. I ripped him out from under the crab right before the crab slammed its body down.

Turning, I bolted down the nearest of the branching paths.

The tunnel twisted and turned, the pale glow from the orb barely illuminating the uneven floor ahead. The relentless scraping and punching against the stone quickened, pursuing me.

Rounding a sharp bend, I slid to a halt. The passage ended abruptly, the rough stone wall blocking any escape.

The blood pounded in my ears. I hugged Tagger tight as I desperately searched for some alternative. Anything.

The cavern walls reverberated with the crab's thunderous charge. My heart hammered faster as the crab's over-sweet stench wafted around the corner.

I set Tagger down. "You're going to have to run," I said grimly. "Don't try to fight." I clicked and snapped my fingers to give him the command. "Do you understand me? Stay away from the crab!"

Tagger bristled, chirping at me sharply.

I pressed my lips into a tight line and shoved the orb back into my pocket. The light became muted, barely enough to see. There were a few rock formations but none high enough to provide full protection. The crab filled the passage. Its eyes glowed, catching the dull light. Its antennae swept in circles.

I dove forward, sliding down to avoid its claw. The stone cracked and cut my legs as I slid. Chitin cracked and splintered beneath the crowbar. The crab scuttled back, striking at me again. The pincher caught the crowbar and yanked it out of my hand.

Gritting my teeth, I spun around just in time to see the spiked claw swinging toward me. Before I could do more than twist to the right behind a series of stalagmites, the crab struck me in the side.

A sickening crack reached my ears along with dull knowledge: I wasn't going to survive this.

Jagged pain cut through me, slicing into my ribcage and blossoming over my side.

All the wind was crushed from my lungs.

I collapsed in a miserable heap.

If the rock formation hadn't taken as much of the force as it did, I would have been dead instantly.

The world spun around me slowly.

The crab loomed over me, the spiked claw lifting.

Tagger screeched. He darted at the crab's legs, nipping and ducking.

My fingers twitched. I tried to feel for the crowbar.

For something.

Anything.

My lungs ached. Stone scraped beneath my fingernails.

Another wave of dizziness swept over me, the pain intensifying.

Nausea roiled within me. I closed my eyes. "Run, Tagger…" I tried to click my tongue at him in case he knew that signal as well.

Tagger jumped onto my chest.

"Ah!" I lost my breath.

Tagger snarled, fluffing up his fur and raising his hackles. He let loose a piercing series of screeches as if cursing the crab and all its spawn.

That high-pitched shriek turned into a roar.

I blinked, trying to lift my head.

What?

"Get away from her!"

A blur of black, green, and yellow leapt over me, the voice booming and echoing off the cavern walls.

Corvin.

He crouched over me and Tagger, snarling at the giant crab. Somehow he seemed even larger now.

The crab swung its claw down again.

Corvin lunged up.

My eyelids dropped.

Heavy rocks crashed. Something snapped.

I struggled to look up again. He'd become an eel, massive

and striped, with vicious jaws. And he was fighting on land? The crab caught him with one claw.

He seized the claw and twisted his head to the side. The claw snapped off with a sickening *crack*.

My eyelids slid shut again. Heavy cracks and blows followed. Tagger's rageful shrieks pierced the air, but they wavered in and out of my consciousness.

The pain in my side grew worse.

My legs. I couldn't move my legs.

Panic rose within me as I struggled for awareness.

Heat spread along my left side, wet and smelling sickly sweet and metallic.

I was going to bleed out soon. But what difference did that make if my legs or back were broken?

Another roar echoed through the passage. Something fell with a sickening crunch.

A hand suddenly grabbed at my face, claws scraping against my cheek. "Don't let go, Mena. Come on. Open your eyes."

I struggled to comply. His face blurred before coming into focus. My lungs weren't filling well.

"Oh…" His face paled more. He lowered my head to the cave floor. "Just—just breathe. It's going to be all right."

Tagger hopped up on the crab's corpse and started striking it with a rock.

"Get down from there," Corvin scolded, glaring at Tagger. "You can eat your fill later. Mena's hurt."

Tagger chucked the rock at Corvin but scurried down. He scrambled up onto my chest again.

Oh! It hurt just as much the second time.

I gasped, all the breath rushing out of my lungs. What little breath had been in them to begin with.

"No." Corvin sighed in frustration, covering his face with

his hand. "Don't sit on her! Where did you learn to comfort people?"

Tagger shook his head and trilled again. He then started rubbing his face against mine. He patted my cheek with his withered paw.

Corvin shook his head again. "What was I thinking?" he muttered. He picked Tagger up and set him down. Then he handed him the pale-blue orb. "Hold this."

My eyelids slid shut again, the heaviness intensifying.

"Hey, don't go to sleep," he said sharply. "I'm furious with you." He lifted my arm from the wound and then swore, his words a garbled mess.

Everything was fading. The cold had moved up over me, far stronger than any pain. A faint cutting sensation and pressure registered in my side. He had put his hand on me again, though stopping the bleeding wouldn't accomplish anything.

A vague panic flared through me as my hearing faded.

This wasn't how I wanted to die.

Down here.

In a cave.

Never seeing Mama again.

But soon I'd see Erryn.

Maybe.

Tears leaked down my cheeks as the cold darkness swallowed me.

HELD

The world rocked. My stomach twisted.

Corvin's voice growled in my ear, hoarse and thick rather than smooth and melodic. "Don't you dare die on me." He cradled me against his chest. "You're much too clever and far too beautiful to just die. You know that, don't you? I'll never forgive you if you die. Don't leave me, clever girl. Please."

I tried to speak, my head spinning. My eyelids refused to cooperate.

Wait.

I was alive.

How?

The pain had mostly gone as well. No wounds or bruises bellowed for attention. All that was really at issue was the cold and fatigue. "What did you do?" I murmured. My eyelids cracked open.

He scoffed, his yellow-and-green striped face paler than usual as he peered down at me. "Saved your sorry hide, you ridiculous creature. For someone so clever, that was foolish. What were you thinking?"

I cringed, startled at how the harshness in his voice stung me. No, not the harshness. The disappointment and the pain.

"Why were you trying to run from me?" he demanded. He shoved the something out of his way, glaring at me.

"I fulfilled my part of the bargain. I came with you to your home."

"And you thought you'd just leave?" He scowled, his breaths rough. "Of course you thought that." Another sharp breath followed, the lines in his face hardening.

My eyelids drifted shut. I tried to lift my leg. My leg resisted, but my toes twitched. The muscles ached. Relief flooded me—then darkness claimed me.

A heavy *thud* roused me along with the smell of old, salted fish.

I startled, my eyes opening just long enough to see he'd gotten me back inside his home and kicked the main door shut. The heavy scratches and gouges in the rock mostly remained, but the ones nearest the lock had vanished.

Murmuring, Corvin took me to the guest room, then hesitated. Gently, he set me on the stone. "Give me a moment." He scooped up my mat and carried it out.

My mouth was dry. Everything ached, but I could feel all my fingers and toes.

I stared up at the ceiling. The fissures and cracks blurred.

Focusing, I twitched my leg again. It responded slowly but without too much pain. Just an ache, as if I had over-worked it. That was something, thank the Creator.

Footsteps scraped across the stone. Corvin returned, lifted me gently, and carried me to his room.

He had placed the two mats together and seemed to have found a third, though it now looked even more like a pile than a bed. After he placed me on them, he slipped a balled-up tunic under my head for a pillow. It smelled like old fabric, stale water, sea salt, and a hint of lavender. "You just need to rest," he said, his voice soft. "You're going to be all right."

Despite his harshness the previous night and the sharpness of his tone moments before, he was startlingly gentle.

The world faded in and out.

He put some sort of foul-tasting liquid to my lips. Then he examined me, his fingers pressing against my arm and side and head and his claws brushing along my flesh. His breath whooshed over my neck and shoulder.

I couldn't keep my eyes open.

He rubbed my hands and wrists, his grip powerful and yet soothing.

"You're like ice," he murmured.

The warmth of his hands around mine was so strong it almost burned, but I couldn't rouse enough to pull away. I just wanted to disappear back into the comfortable haze of sleep, yet questions provoked me despite my exhaustion. They nibbled at my mind, demanding answers.

He'd saved me somehow.

I tried to speak, but my tongue was like a brick in my mouth. A small attempt at asking how resulted in a garbled string of syllables.

"Wasn't going to let you die," he grumbled in response. He pulled my shoes and the oversized socks off. Then he mumbled something about it being too cold and how he hadn't realized it. He rubbed my feet and ankles, scowling.

I winced slightly. Despite his claws, he handled me with care, pressing and massaging to get the blood flowing. It stung and ached, yet also felt incredible. Painfully good.

He continued to mutter and growl, but sweet night, the man knew how to get the blood flowing again. His hands moved along my feet and calves with steady intensity, working away the knots and forcing the blood through.

Sometimes his claws lightly scraped my skin, sending shudders of pleasure through me at the stimulation.

Though I cringed, I didn't fight him or kick. Not even when his claws brushed that ticklish line down the center of each of my feet.

It was the first time in ages someone had actually taken care of me.

I swallowed hard, the weariness still pulling me down. This was horrible. I should hate him. Except—honestly—it was really hard to even dislike someone who was this skilled at making me feel good.

It's just—I knew I should hate him.

"You're sleeping in my bed tonight," he said. "With me. It's too cold for you to be in the guest room. There's no heat here." The last words had a bitter note to them. "No heat anywhere." He continued to rub my ankles, his grip strong and firm. "But I'm not letting you die from the cold. Or anything else."

"How am I not dead?" I murmured.

"You just aren't. Rest. We can talk tomorrow." He massaged my feet a few minutes longer and then lay down beside me, pulling up the blankets over us.

"Hmmph," I protested.

"We both know you're cold," he growled. "I'm not going to hurt you. But I am going to keep you warm."

"Fine." I set my jaw.

He pulled me close and wrapped his arms around me.

It was all I could do to keep from gasping.

Oh, salt's bane!

I hated myself now instead of him. Hated how much I enjoyed his arms around me and even the smell of him. He smelled more of salt water than the cologne he had worn before, and his body wrapped completely around me, burying me in blissful heat and comfort.

I was a traitor to my mother and to my own independence, because right now all I wanted was to be held.

He tucked his chin over the top of my head. "How do you feel?" he demanded. "Am I hurting you?" His voice was so much rougher than before, vibrating through me. A faint tremor passed through his arms.

"No," I admitted reluctantly.

"Good." He burrowed a little closer. "I just—I just want you to be all right." He adjusted the blankets and extra garments over us. His hand pressed against my side where the wound had been.

Had been.

It didn't even hurt now.

He pressed his cheek to mine, his voice a low rumble. "You're not in pain." I couldn't tell whether it was a question or a statement. "It's not coming back."

"Should it?" I tensed as his hands pressed along my side to my waist and stomach and along my hip.

Tagger hopped up on us and curled up like a cat, draped over our sides. His whiskers tickled my cheek.

A long pause followed. "No...it shouldn't." His voice softened. "You're safe." He hugged me closer. "You're safe, Mena."

Was I?

A long silence passed.

Maybe I really did feel safe. Even with his claws lightly pressed into my arm and his foot tucked over mine. His body was like granite behind me, but it was soothing as well.

Sleep claimed me before I could torment myself further.

A cold, wet snout poked my cheek. Warm, fishy breath filled my nose.

Wincing, I opened my eyes to find Tagger staring into my eyes. He booped me and then hopped back, his tiny black claws and coarse paw pads making soft claps on the stone floor.

I sat up slowly, my body not nearly as stiff or sore as I expected. I guessed the healing that had kept me from dying yesterday had finished its process and made me better than when I started.

The door was slightly ajar.

I stood. My knees and spine cracked, and when I stretched, it felt wonderful. Tagger hopped near the doorway, urging me to come out.

I complied.

To my surprise, Corvin had prepared something special.

The table had been set with several items: a plate of salted fish, fresh out of a tin of oil so that the filets shone in the pale-blue light, a couple scratched jars of pickled vegetables of some sort, a leaf-wrapped bread that was falling apart, a tall, striped pitcher without a handle, and a cracked stone plate.

Corvin placed a couple battered serving utensils on the table before turning to face me. He wore the same black garb as yesterday, the garments immaculate and crisp, and his boots shiny.

"I made you breakfast," he said, his demeanor somber. Something was bothering him. He held a large mug in his left hand. His gaze was downcast. Three deep lines formed over his brow.

"Thank you." I folded my hands in front of myself as I approached the table.

"It's not much," he said. "I know the pickled vegetables are safe to eat. And the fish. I—I suppose I don't know about the bread. It's salt pumpernickel, and it was wrapped in leaves. But it was cracked. It's…salty."

A small smile tugged at my mouth. "Thank you." I brushed my fingertips over the tabletop. "And thank you for helping me. How did you heal me?"

He scowled, the lines in his brow deepening. "It was nothing. The medicine. That's all. That's what it was."

Something in the way he said that made me even more suspicious. Something had happened. Something he hadn't expected and wouldn't explain.

Even stranger, I wanted to be close to him again. I curled my fingers against my palms, steadying myself. Then I drew in a deep breath. "I thought I was dead."

Raw emotion cut through his eyes, darkening the brightness. "Well, you aren't."

"How, though?"

His throat bobbed. "Just…"

It was significant then.

I stared at him hard, folding my arms. "How did you heal that wound? It felt like that spike on the crab's claw tore me. I…I felt myself going cold. I was bleeding out. And I couldn't move my legs. I think—I think I broke my back. I was paralyzed and bleeding out. Wasn't I?"

He grabbed a jar from the cupboard and made another mug of the strange herbal concoction. It smelled foul but familiar. "Yeah," he murmured, his gaze fixed on me and his frown still present. He drank the cold, murky liquid.

"So what happened?" I approached him, then flinched. Where had I smelled that before?

"I healed you. Accidentally."

"Seems like a really lucky accident."

He grunted, then finished the mug of whatever herbal concoction he was drinking. "I have duties to attend to. Tagger will stay with you. There's dried and salted salmon if you want it. And whatever else you find in here."

I nodded, rubbing my arm as I contemplated what he said.

"Don't try to run this time." He removed his cloak and handed it to me. "To keep you warm. You can explore the rest of the rooms here. Use anything you like. But don't leave. All right? I—I'll see about doing something to make it warmer."

I accepted the cloak but twitched my shoulders noncommittally.

"Promise me," he said, sterner this time. His bright-green eyes darkened. "You can't get to the surface through the cave anyway. Those vents that you're smelling the air from aren't big enough for anyone to get through. All access points are below the sea, and there are more giant crabs in there among other things. Plus it's a maze."

I narrowed my eyes at him.

He responded in kind. "Promise me that you will stay here until I return, and I will go check on your mother. There's a storm right now, but I can make sure she's safe."

"Another storm? How bad is it?" My arms dropped to my sides.

He shrugged. "Bad enough that they can't get any signals out. And the boundary's still got them trapped, so even if another ship does come by, they can't get anywhere. Yet."

"So they're just out there, alone in the cold?"

"No." He pinched the bridge of his nose. "There is shelter on the island. They aren't the first to be trapped there. Just… trust me. I'll make sure your mother is safe. All right?"

"Fine. I promise then."

"Thank you." He sighed, then pulled the cloak up around my shoulders. "I'll be back soon."

I watched him leave. Tagger hopped up on the table beside me. He tilted his head and squeaked.

"I never thanked you for helping me." I held out my hand. When he sniffed my fingers, I scratched him. His fur was every bit as soft and dense as it looked. As I offered him some of the fish, I smiled at him. He snatched it out of my hands and gobbled it up.

I didn't touch the water-logged bread. The dwarves were

able to eat that kind of bread even after it fell into the ocean, but I wasn't certain it wouldn't make me sick.

Instead I tried a few pieces of the greasy fish and some of the pickled vegetables: pickled mushrooms, pickled green beans, pickled onions, and pickled beets. Not the most appetizing, but the sharp, vinegary flavor reminded me of hot summer days when my family had been whole and the family table had been loaded with the summer harvest. Even when I was working at the tavern and Erryn had been fighting against giving up her dream of being a singer, it hadn't been so bad. Bowls of fresh greens, deviled eggs, loaves of egg-washed wheat bread, tureens of steaming soup.

Cooking had been one of the few things in those final days that Erryn, Mama, and I could all do together. Sure, we tended to fight somewhere between peeling the carrots, chopping the onions, and kneading the bread. But usually by the time the table was full and the blue taper candles lit, we had settled our differences enough or someone had cracked a joke to clear the air.

My breath caught in my throat. I pressed my hand to my cheeks, pushing back the tears that welled up.

Those days were gone.

Maybe I could convince Corvin to let me go.

He wasn't nearly as dreadful or frightening as he might be, and the way he had held me last night...my heart stuttered. I swallowed hard. As much as I wanted to see Mama again and hug her, a sort of pain struck me at the thought of leaving Corvin.

This place wasn't good.

It was miserable and wretched.

Surely he'd find the idea of a new life and new home at least tempting.

Tagger thrust his snout against my hand again, asking for pets.

"Maybe both you and Corvin could come with me," I murmured as I gave him the belly rub he requested. He squeaked in pure happiness, wriggling on the table for a few minutes until at last he had had enough.

Now to decide what I was going to do with my time down here.

I crossed to the nearest of the locked doors and tested the handle. This time it yielded at once. The door creaked open. I peered inside.

My eyes widened, my hand flying to my mouth. "What!"

HEAT

This wasn't just a room. It was a cavern. A cavern stuffed with…things.

The cavern stretched beyond sight, lit with small pale-blue orbs near the entrance. As I stepped farther in, I realized there were additional chambers. Inside this place were all manner of items from various wrecks. Some must have been from the *Seaforger's Pride*, because they were still drying out: strips of cloth, crates of food, broken boxes, books laid out on flat surfaces. All tossed in without any organization.

He just collected things and laid them out here to dry before figuring out what to do with them.

I raised an eyebrow. From the looks of it, he never figured out what to do with half of it. And there was wood. Lots and lots of wood. Enough to be a fire hazard if anyone managed to get a flame ablaze in here.

Tagger trotted in after me. He scuffled about and rubbed his chin on a broken bit of green pottery. As he scurried along, he slipped between a shattered crate and a broken chair.

There was just so much in here. Corvin must have been gathering these items for years. How long had he lived in this place?

The dripping of water was the only sound aside from my own breathing to disturb the space. It was hard to take it all in. I paused as I glimpsed a familiar shape in the middle of the first storeroom, a large swell of black metal.

"Son of a scallop. He's got a whole woodstove!" I set my hands on my waist and shook my head, sighing. The man had brought in a whole woodstove. Not just one or two. Three! One was so large I had no idea how he got it in here unless he dragged it in while in his eel form. His jaws had to have ached holding that metal beast.

The second was worth little more than scrap metal.

But the third was an old dwarven woodstove intended for travel, whether in ships or on wagons. It was sturdy but manageable, similar to one I'd encountered many times over the past years.

The dark grey woodstove was not as heavy as some I had seen. It had been made with a particular type of dwarven steel that was far lighter and more durable than the iron that was used in the tavern where I first worked. One side had been dented, and the door hung crooked. But, with a fair bit of huffing, grunting, and shoving, I moved the woodstove out into the main room.

The air flow was the next thing to manage. There were numerous holes and vents in the ceiling and walls that might work. So I tested each one until I found a couple that would suffice. From there, I started putting up the pipes from all three of the wood stoves, having to fit them together and twist them.

In this way, the day passed slowly but almost pleasantly. The last time I had put together one of these stoves, it had been in a ramshackle halfway house that served as a tavern, a general store, a flower shop, and a tiny hospital. Mama had been too busy with her translations and notes to see all the work that went into it, but I had been proud of myself for managing to fix the stove and pipes with precious little help from anyone.

Not that I blamed them. The shifters were dealing with a condition that sent them into rapid shifting. They had to take medicine regularly just to keep their human forms.

Tagger, at least, vocalized his appreciation of my actions. He chirped as he trailed along behind me, investigating each pipe and circling the stove multiple times.

I searched through the crates and found several items, including a dented pot. Ingredients were even easier to find, including some mostly fresh produce like potatoes, celery, carrots, sweet potatoes, onions, and garlic. Lots and lots of pickled and preserved foods, mostly intact though a few jars were cracked. Some sealed jars and tins of spices and herbs had made it through as well. I carried them all out to the table and then dragged out some of the wood he had gathered.

The wood near the front was either damp or soaked. But the pieces farther in the cavern were dry and brittle. I hauled these out. Then I fished out the bit of flint from the ring with my special spoon.

Within minutes, a fire blazed in the woodstove. And the pipes sent the smoke out into the farther depths of the cave. A little of the smoky scent filled the chamber, but that just improved the overall odor.

Feeling better, I changed back into my own dress, the mauve fabric stiff and uncomfortable but familiar. As I did, my fingers brushed over the little book I'd taken from Mama's desk. My heart clenched.

Mama.

Gently, I lifted the wet book and studied it. My fingers traced the delicate lines and fragile pages. It wasn't in as bad of a condition as I'd expected, probably because it had been made and treated for researchers who worked on the seas. Some of the ink had run in a few places, but the vast majority was legible.

The book naturally fell open to the spot I had last been reading. The part about the grounded staircases that led into the air and how they were not as dangerous to use as the ones that randomly appeared. There were several scattered throughout the world that still had the necessary grounding runes and mechanisms to work. And a grounded staircase could be used to create a portal that would connect to another grounded staircase with a portal.

I bit the inside of my lip, remembering my last words.

Guilt rose within me. My shoulders sagged.

I carried the book out to the kitchen and set it down so that the heat would reach it.

Tagger nudged it.

"Leave that alone." I adjusted the ties of my apron. "I need to get dinner started." As I started to organize my working space, I sighed. "Obviously, I'll make something with fish. I'd love it if I could get fresh fish. Ironic, isn't it? We're under the ocean, and the only fish I can find is that horrible salted stuff. I do have some cured smoked sausage, so that will help. But this is going to be so salty if I'm not careful."

Tagger padded toward the door that led out to the water entry. He pressed his paw against the runes and then passed through the small flap door set at the base.

My brows lifted. So that was how he did it!

Crossing over, I tested the door handle. It did not give at all. Nor did the little door at the base that Tagger had gone through. It was probably enchanted just for him.

Shaking my head, I returned to my little makeshift kitchen and started to prepare the stew. The well in the back corner provided plenty of clean water. The dirty water, I dumped into the waste chamber in the wash room. Over the course of the next hour, I seared onions, garlic, celery, and carrots. No flour to make a roux, unfortunately. But the savory fragrance was enough to make my mouth water and remind me of the tavern and of home.

Tagger brought in a large silver snapper. He dropped it at my feet.

My eyes widened. "Oh...that—you understood me?" Why was I even surprised?

He chirped happily, then darted out again before I could thank him.

By the time I finished cleaning the first fish, Tagger had returned with another snapper. The third time, he came back with something similar to tilapia. I scaled and chopped the fish, leaving the heads, fins, and scales in a yellow bowl. He hopped up on the same stool and scooped up the top fish head, devouring it with contented chirps.

It was hard to tell how much time had passed, but it had to be at least a few hours. Maybe several.

The stew simmered beneath the dented lid, and I had gathered the rest of the necessary items for a nice evening meal as well as chopped and stacked a sufficient quantity of wood. The cave had become pleasantly toasty, and the air smelled like garlic, snapper, tomatoes, and spices.

I stirred the stew with my special spoon, my fingers settling nicely in the familiar carved runes. I breathed in the steam and sighed, a pang of homesickness and a yearning for times long past sweeping over me.

The door scraped open across the stone.

Tagger shrieked with delight and bolted off the crooked chair, fish head tucked against his chest.

Corvin stood in the doorway, a bewildered expression on his face and his brows knit. "What did you do?"

The look of utter shock on his face made my smile crooked. I tapped the spoon on the side of the dinged pot. "I made a few changes. Partially because they were needed. And partially to say thank you for saving me." And partially to help convince him that he needed to let me go. I couldn't stay here.

Once again, the thought of leaving him struck me. Harder this time. I soothed it with a promise to ask him if he would go with me.

"How did you make it burn?" He crouched down beside the woodstove, setting his hand on the stone behind it as he peered inside at the flames with something like reverence. "I've tried...so many times."

"I had flint with me."

He glanced up at me, his expression soft, almost vulnerable. "It's warm in here now."

Something in the small way he smiled cut my heart. He just remained there, crouched, staring at it. "How did you move this stove in here? It's heavy."

"I'm stronger than I look," I declared, smiling. "I bet if I needed to, I could carry you." As he scoffed good-naturedly, I shook my head. "I could."

"I'm heavier than this woodstove by a long shot," he said.

"And I am far stronger than I look." I glanced back at him, those threads inside me plucking as I looked at him. "So you've never had any heat? Ever?"

"We don't do fire in this place. There are hot water streams. Especially in the King of the North Sea's actual home. But not where I live. The caves stay fairly constant in their temperature year round." He stared at the flickering flames and the glowing wood. "I didn't even know fire existed until—well, until one of the ships caught fire during a storm. It was an oil fire."

"How long have you lived here?"

"Oh…years now. As soon as I was old enough to hold the eel form, they put me here." He ran his hand along the edge of the wood stove. "It's hard to keep track of time down here."

"And you've always been alone?" I knew the answer as soon as I asked it. But it had slipped out nonetheless.

"I'm an enforcer. Enforcers aren't allowed to have mates. And these are the outskirts of the North Sea. I'm fortunate enough to have shelter and a purpose," he said quietly. He pulled his hand back and looked down at it, his fingers pressing against the clawed bracelet that was set against his flesh.

Something inside me clenched. I wanted to ask more, but before I could, he turned his gaze to me. "You really are remarkable with your problem solving, clever girl."

Heat rose to my cheeks at once. I at once took my special spoon and scooped up the stew into one of the bowls. "It's nothing." Discomfort at the compliment clipped my words. "Now come on. We should eat before it gets cold." My gaze drifted back to him. He was still looking at me. The moment our eyes met, sharper heat and tightness spasmed through me. My cheeks had to be bright red by now. "How are you able to get dry so fast?" I stumbled over my words.

He held my gaze a moment longer, his eyes bright and yet vulnerable. Then he cleared his throat. "It's a shifter fae trick, but it isn't always reliable." He ran his hand through his thick hair, finally breaking away. "Sometimes I accidentally destroy what I'm trying to dry."

"Destroy it? How?" I scowled, raising an eyebrow.

"It turns to dust. I've lost whole outfits that way." He straightened and took the bowl from my hands. He carried it to the table. "I don't have complete control over my shifting all the time. Part of—well, just part of who I am." He set it down and then crossed back to me as Tagger trailed along. "It smells...incredible."

"If you can't have fire, what do you do for cooking food? Do you just dry it?"

"The only time we eat hot food is when we're in the king's court. They have streams of hot water there and lava vents," he said, his voice tight.

I ladled the thick stew into a second bowl, making sure to add a little extra of the savory red broth. "Well, now you can have hot food here." I set my special wooden spoon down. The silence barely breathed between us before I launched into my own question. I couldn't handle any quiet right now. "Why do you have all this stuff if you don't use it? There's almost enough there to build a whole ship." Was he maybe trying to escape on his own?

"You never know when you'll need it," he said with a shrug. "I don't know what a fair bit of it's for. But it seemed wasteful to leave it." He took the second bowl from me and carried it to the table. "You didn't have to do this. It was a lot of effort."

"It benefits me as much as you." I tried to sound casual. My heart raced faster. I paused as he pulled out the chair for me. "Oh. Um. Thank you."

I sat slowly, realizing that the place he had chosen for me was where he had put the first bowl of stew. He'd served me first. "Were you able to find my mother?"

He took a spoonful of the stew. "She was resting in the shelter," he said. "I didn't want to wake her." His eyes widened as he took a bite. "This...this is incredible." He took another bite, then gasped as he burned his tongue. Shaking his head, he gulped down mouthfuls of water. Then he cleared his throat. "They said she was fine. It was the captain I spoke with. He was at the meeting point. So I gave him your message, and he promised to tell your mother when she woke. I think that storm is going to keep them there for a while longer."

I paused. "How did Hosvir know to meet you there?"

He lifted his head from his stew, startled. "What?"

NOT MY MATE

I frowned. Why was he so surprised at that question? "You said he was at the meeting point. Why did you have an established meeting point?"

"Um…" He cleared his throat, his back now straight. "It was the point at which we met. Not so much a formal place. I saw him, and I remembered that he seemed to care for your mother. Which he does. And so I asked him, and I gave him the message. He promised to give it to her. It's not really anything special. Then I handled my other tasks for the king. This is delicious." He cleared his throat, staring down once more at the bowl of stew. His shoulders dropped. "I didn't realize how…bad this place was until you were here." He shoveled another bite in his mouth.

"Really? Don't you feel the cold?" Damn it. It had just slipped out. I shook my head, dipping my chin down. Now I needed to change the topic, though I made a note to return to what had happened with Mama and Hosvir. Something felt off about his story. Not that he hadn't met with Hosvir. Somehow, I knew that part was true. But the part about the meeting place was not. "I'm sorry. I just—sometimes I say things—"

"No. It's true. It's always cold. It's not pleasant. It didn't occur to me that you wouldn't do well down here." He paused. "Maybe that's why..." He paused, considering something.

"Why what?" My curiosity prickled.

"Humans are forbidden in my home."

"Just humans?" I took a bite of the stew, savoring the soothing richness of the savory broth and the bite of the tomatoes mixed with the fish. "I'd have thought it being under the sea would make that almost redundant."

He shrugged. "They're forbidden in some of the other enforcer and shifter fae homes as well. But all enforcers are forbidden from having a certain species in their quarters. For me, it's humans. Usually it isn't an issue. Dwarves, elves, and fae are more likely to travel these paths. You're the first human I ever saw." He laughed a little.

I laughed as well. "I suppose that makes sense. Though complimenting me on being the prettiest girl you'd seen suddenly seems far less impressive and much more understandable."

"Oh. No." He set his spoon down as he stared at me. "You're the first female human I've seen. But I've seen and spoken with many other females, including princesses and duchesses and the like. You are incomparable. If all women were like you, I'd imagine the king would tell us to not even look upon any vessel carrying a human instead of just telling me I can't have human guests."

My hands dropped into my lap, and my face burned. What could I even say to that? And he wasn't even smirking. He'd said it so sincerely, so openly. As if it were entirely true without hesitation or limitation. "I—why would there be different requirements for different enforcers?"

He resumed eating, devouring the stew hungrily. "The King of the North Sea doesn't like to be questioned. It's always been this way. When I was officially required to enter his service, I received certain instructions. Some of them saved my life. Others—well, I'm certain he has his reasons. It's not for me to question." He said the last part like he struggled to convince himself more than me.

"Saved your life?"

"I'm diseased." He said it flatly, the words just hanging there for a moment. "Not contagious or anything, fortunately. But diseased. It's why my family abandoned me."

I almost dropped the spoon. "Your family—"

"Yes. I don't want to talk about it." His voice had gone hard. He stared down at his stew, then shook his head. "I was a child. I don't even remember them. They looked at me and decided they didn't want me. But I am cursed or diseased or whatever you prefer to call whatever this is." He gestured toward his appearance. "I can become an eel. That's basically it."

"You were a mer," I said, the words slipping out more to fill the silence than because they were important.

He gave a rough shrug, then took another bite of stew. His shoulders remained tense. "It's in between the human and eel forms. Only good thing about it is I'm really good in the form I have. I'm very strong, and I can endure a lot. All the rest who are diseased like me, we have that going for us, I guess. Even though we'd give almost anything to be full shifters like we're supposed to be. At least we serve a purpose here. Though, sometimes, what bothers me the most is that I can't even change what I look like in my state of rest. I always have these cursed stripes." He gestured toward his face.

His striping pattern *was* unusual. I wasn't sure what to say. And if I opened my mouth, I'd probably say something stupid like how much I liked yellow and green.

He continued, his voice darker and harsher. "I shouldn't forget my place though. I'm grateful to have a place to live, wretched as it can be sometimes. It's dangerous in some parts for shifter fae to be so visible. They're always killing us beyond the North Sea's boundaries. Skinning us. Enslaving us. They use us for potions and labor. We have to blend in, or else we die."

I frowned at this. That wasn't what I had seen with shifter fae at all. Shifter fae were incredibly hard to defeat. Many were warriors and mercenaries. Most I had seen could become more than one creature. There had been one guide who helped Mama and me across the Painted Mountain Pass, and he had been capable of transforming into a mountain lion, a grizzly bear, and a fanged squirrel among other things. My fingers curled against my palm. "Who would do such a thing?"

"Many out there hate shifter fae, especially ones like me," he said. "The King of the North Sea alone offers us shelter and an opportunity to make something of ourselves. If not for him, I would have had nothing and been nothing. But because of him, I am an enforcer." These words sounded as if he had said them many times. "He was gracious to us, even though he was imprisoned."

I considered this, nibbling on my lip. This didn't make sense. And everyone else spoke of the King of the North Sea as if he were some terrible monster, not a great benefactor who would offer refuge to persecuted shifter fae. "I don't know why he was imprisoned in the North Sea. Only that something dreadful happened years and years ago. Long before my time. But I've seen many shifter fae in my travels. Shifters with striping similar to yours too."

He stiffened, his arm still resting on the tabletop. "You have? Living shifter fae?"

I nodded. "Past the Painted Mountain Pass there was a

village that was almost all shifter fae. None of them had green and yellow stripes like you exactly, but there were some who were...well...very colorful. One man had turquoise skin with red triangles and silver lines. And another had deep-blue skin that sometimes glowed."

"This was an unusual place?"

I shook her head. "Not really. They said that a number of their residents were travelers. But those who lived there seemed happy. There were several different cadres, some of them quite large."

"Children too?" His brow furrowed. His claws dug into the table, making it shift on the uneven leg. "Were there children in that place? Were there—were there bright children?"

I nodded. "Yes. There were more in a fishing village just before we set sail. Duke's Port. Probably less than two weeks' swim for you. You could go visit them."

"I am not permitted." He gripped his wrist, his hand folding over the claw bracelet. His sleeve almost hid it.

"Convenient," I mused. But a little bit of hope flared within me. He could come with me. He probably would. Even if he wasn't allowed, he'd be tempted to join me. I knew he would. Then he could meet other shifters and maybe find a cure.

He crossed to the woodstove and counter. "If not for the king, I'd be dead." He then picked up a mug and removed the jar of herbs from the cupboard.

Tagger watched him, gnawing on the fish head as he sat on his stool.

"That's kind of funny," I mused. "You were able to heal me somehow, but you have to drink that concoction for your disease?" I crossed over and took the jar from his hand.

His eyebrows lifted. He shrugged then. "I suppose so."

I sniffed the herbs, then winced. The foul scent struck me even harder now. It was definitely familiar. Back at that ramshackle place…several of the shifter fae had drank something similar. But it wasn't medicine exactly. They had sat by the fire and sipped it to keep themselves from losing their forms. Slippery root, snake's bane, and glory cabbage. "What exactly does this do to help you? This smells like something the shifter fae in the village used to suppress shifter instincts."

"Hmm." He shrugged at that and took another grimacing sip. "Makes sense, I suppose. If I don't take it, then it advances, and it will shred me within hours. I'll lose my ability to hold myself together. So it probably is suppressing that. It certainly makes me feel more…solid. Less like I'm about to fall apart. Maybe that's why I can only become the eel."

That sounded awful. "You have to drink a lot of it."

"Not until recently. I used to take one mug every three days." He managed another sip. "Past couple days…it's just gotten worse."

I frowned. That sounded…bad. "It will—it will kill you?"

"If I stop taking the medicinal herbs, probably." He took another long drink. "Don't worry," he said dryly. "I already put in a request for added stores. The king is good at ensuring we are never without a supply. I know…" He paused, as if something had occurred to him.

"So you were able to heal me, but it doesn't work for you?"

His gaze darted back to me. "No…I mean, yes." His scowl deepened. "I don't know what happened. Most shifter fae can't do that. Not unless they're healers. I'm not a healer. So that's not what happened." He took a drink and grimaced, shaking his head.

"They can't heal anyone? That doesn't sound right." I shook my head as I watched him. "I saw one shifter fae heal another. He got mauled by a bear. Didn't look like he was going to make it."

He scowled, then scoffed. "Were they mated?"

"Possibly?" I managed a small, nervous laugh. "I didn't exactly ask their relationship status."

"Shifter fae can heal their mates." His bright-green eyes had gone sharp and hungry again, piercing me through.

He had healed me.

My stomach somersaulted. Wait—was that why I was feeling this way? "Are you saying—"

"I don't have a mate," he said, his voice rough. "And even if I did, I wouldn't be allowed to take a mate. If I were found with my mate, I would be executed and so would she." He raked his hand through his hair, the words just spilling out. "Mating bonds happen fast," he said, his voice low. "If I could have a mate, I would have known if you were mine as soon as I touched you. But I can't have a mate. And I—"

"You didn't feel anything for me?" I folded my arms. What was even wrong with me for feeling hurt at that statement? I didn't want him to have feelings for me. Of course not!

The way he looked at me though... He wasn't the first man to look at me in a way similar to this. But he was the most intense. "Fine then." I wasn't going to push it. It wasn't as if I wanted him thinking lustful thoughts about me or feeling me up.

My cheeks heated as I tried to avoid imagining his hands roaming over my body and the light strokes of his claws on my flesh. That was not what I wanted. Not at all!

The tension that radiated through my body was nothing more than...my mind blanked as I struggled to come up with an excuse. It wasn't real! And I wasn't disappointed. I was just —lonely. Salt's bane, I hated myself.

Then I realized he was still staring at me. His throat bobbed.

"You didn't feel anything for me, did you?" I asked again, softer this time.

"Are you telling me you did?"

His gaze pinned me in place. There was—there was something. Was it a mate bond?

"Listen. Let's not pretend. There's no mate bond before us. And I should be glad there isn't. The herbs are tailored to my blood as it is. If you were my mate, our connection would change even my blood. And the medicine wouldn't work."

"So you'd die?"

He paused, then shook his head. "Well, yeah, if I could have a mate. But I can't. That's the whole thing with this disease. Everything the King of the North Sea does is targeted at our blood and our core. A mate bond would change that. Finding a mate would be more than just—" He stopped, his brow pinching. "This is pointless. I grabbed you because I was lonely and I liked you. And the only reason you agreed to come with me was to ensure your mother and the crew survived. You didn't feel a mate bond."

"Of course not. I'm not a shifter fae. I'm not a fae at all. I'm just an ordinary human. I'm a spinster stew cook." The words snapped out, harsher than I intended. I tried to swallow the knot of emotion that built within me. "There's nothing special about me."

He hissed through his teeth. "Don't speak of yourself that way. Just because your mother cannot see your value beyond her use for you does not mean you have no value."

"Don't speak about my mother." My chest tightened.

He finished the murky liquid and set the mug down hard. Grimacing, he wiped his mouth. "You're going to ask me to let you go, aren't you?"

I struggled to calm my heart. This wasn't going the way I'd planned. My stomach twisted. "I don't see any reason for you to keep me here. If you're just lonely, I'll find a way to send you letters or something. But my mother needs me." My voice faltered before I could suggest he come with me. He didn't allow the pause to rest.

"Your mother only cares about finding your sister, and you said yourself that your sister is likely dead." He waved his hand as he served himself more stew.

I had lost my appetite, so I took my bowl and dropped it in the washbasin full of cold water. I hated that he was right. "My mother can't do this alone. She's lost everything…"

"So have you. Why do you insist on defending her? She treated you horribly. You have taken care of her all these years. You have looked after her. She does not protect you. She simply weeps and mourns for the daughter lost to her years ago." He jabbed his finger at me. "You are worth more than that, woman. I have only known you for a few days, but I know that. Just because you are not my mate does not mean I cannot see just how valuable and brilliant you are. How much better you deserve."

"So you want to keep me trapped down here in a cave under the sea forever?" I set my hands on my waist, glaring at him even as my heart felt like it was splitting. No one had ever spoken to me in this way. Yelling was common enough. But he sounded like he saw me and cared.

His brow furrowed. His shoulders dropped. "Mena…"

"Don't speak ill of my family if you want to keep talking to me," I said.

He raised an eyebrow. "But you have said—"

"I can talk about my family. You can't."

His shoulders dropped, his voice softening. "Why would you want to go back with them, though? I will pay attention to you. You may not be my mate, but I—I—" He broke off before he could finish the thought.

My eyes widened. Had he been about to say he loved me? My mouth went dry.

No. That wasn't possible. We hadn't known each other long enough. I had to stop being ridiculous. And even if he had been about to say it—well, I wasn't a shifter fae. I still needed time. Didn't I?

A loud splash sounded outside the door to the water entry. Heavy footsteps followed. Then a loud thudding struck the door. "Enforcer Corvin, answer," a deep voice bellowed.

Tagger hopped off the stool, squeaking and bristling.

Corvin's attention snapped to me, his expression hard. "You have to hide. Now," he growled.

INTERROGATED

I didn't know who was coming or why, but my instincts warned me it was bad.

I snatched Mama's little book off the corner of the table and dropped my glass and spoon in the washbasin with the bowl before Corvin grabbed my arm.

He dragged me to one of the large shelves, opened a sliding panel in the back, picked me up, and shoved me inside. I startled, not even realizing that the shelves had false backs. A smuggler's ship must have wrecked in these waters.

"No matter what happens, don't say a word. No matter what. Not even if they attack me. If they find out you're here, you'll never see your mother again," he hissed. Then he pulled the panel shut. A small crack allowed me to peer out.

Another pounding knock struck the door. The rune marks on it flared bright yellow. "Answer!"

Corvin raked his hand through his hair and then opened the door. "You feel the need to interrupt my rest?" He demanded, faking sleepiness in his voice.

Three fae shoved inside. The largest, a broad-shouldered warrior with glistening embellishments and epaulets over light leather, entered first. He had thick silver-green hair and dark-green eyes. His teeth were sharp, and his heavy-veined hands had claws. He strode in, the metal on his shoulders and his belt clinking with each heavy step.

My heart pounded. This man was bad news. I bit the inside of my lip as I stared through the crack.

One of the smaller fae had wings like fins folded against his back. His skin was purple and blue with sharp blue ridges along his cheeks and actual gold worked into his flesh. He shoved Corvin hard as a third fae with solid black eyes and black claws slammed the door shut.

Corvin staggered back, his expression hard. "What do you want, Lishen?" he demanded, his gaze fixed on the largest of the three.

Tagger bristled, his hackles shooting up. He trilled and chattered. Black Claws moved to kick him.

Corvin darted in front of Tagger, not deflecting the blow but taking it instead. He didn't even flinch when the fae's boot connected with his leg, but he bared his teeth at Black Claws. "Touch the otter, and I—"

Lishen struck Corvin across the face, knocking him to the ground.

I cringed, covering my mouth.

Corvin hit the ground hard. Tagger shook his head, hissing and squeaking. He stomped his paws like he was about to attack. But Corvin snapped his fingers at him. "Away, Tagger!" He pushed himself up, wiping the blood from his mouth.

Tagger looked at him, his dark eyes sparkling. Then he bolted under the table.

"Leave the pet alone," Lishen ordered coldly. He clicked his tongue at Corvin as he stood. "You know why we're here."

Corvin pressed his hand to his mouth. He was still bleeding, but there was murder in his eyes as he stared at Lishen. "I do not know. I have already been to the king and answered his questions."

Lishen strode farther into the room, his gaze narrowing as it fell upon the woodstove. "You have made some changes to your residence."

Corvin glared but gave a slight nod. "I also made food."

"You had company?" Lishen gestured toward the washbasin with the second bowl and glass.

Corvin shrugged. "I ate. Then I went to rest, realized I was hungry again and needed to take the medicine. So I got another bowl. Stew's still hot."

Lishen's eyes narrowed. He chuckled, shaking his head. He dipped his finger in the bowl, then nodded. "So it is. I didn't know you had the skill." He drew in a deep breath. "You've been full of surprises." He set his arms akimbo as he strode back. "And we do not like surprises, Corvin."

"I am not aware of any surprises," Corvin answered, his voice low and deadly. Tagger watched with glittering eyes from behind Corvin, teeth still bared. "All has been as it should be."

"Except it hasn't. This last wreck. There are survivors on the island. And they aren't dead. They aren't even close to dead. The leviathans should be hungry. Yet they were sated. As if they had devoured all aboard the vessel, the way it should be. And someone saw you speaking with a dwarf captain."

"I warned him that if he stepped into the waters again while the boundary encompassed the island, he and all with him would die. His luck will not hold out a second time."

Lishen wagged his finger, a slight smile curling at his lips. Black Claws and Blue Ridges started searching the cavern. They opened the doors and the cupboards, rattling about noisily. Black Claws flung open the bedroom door as Blue Ridges searched the guest room.

I held my breath, grateful I hadn't left anything in there. Nothing except my spoon on the woodstove. My stomach twisted.

Corvin remained motionless as Lishen stepped in front of him.

"So you have never met the dwarf captain before?" Lishen asked, his voice almost sickeningly sweet.

"Not that I am aware of," Corvin said calmly. He folded his arms over his chest, his head tilting. His voice had taken a hard edge. "But many have come and gone over the years. I only concern myself with those on ships that stray beyond the boundary and those who require warnings. I do not worry myself with remembering those who live or die. Why burden myself with the useless?"

"Hmmm. Except I am certain I saw that dwarf before. The green and indigo kraken tattoos…they are distinct. Are they not?"

Corvin shrugged. "I don't concern myself with such things."

"What do you concern yourself with?" Lishen demanded.

More dishes clattered and broke. Black Claws started pulling items out of the cupboard by the woodstove. Blue Ridges flung the mats out from the bedroom and ripped one of the blankets in half. The ragged tear of fabric dragged out as Lishen stared Corvin down.

"I concern myself with my duties. I have fulfilled all of them to the letter," Corvin said coldly. "I am charged with ensuring that ships violating the boundary are destroyed. The ship was destroyed. Every ship that has crossed the boundary has been destroyed."

"There was a young woman," Lishen said softly. "A human woman. Where is she, Corvin?"

He gave a bewildered grunt that was actually convincing. His expression remained like granite, blood leaking from his lips, his eyes dead. "Drowned, most likely."

"Strange. All those survivors. And the only one missing is a very pretty human female."

"The sea has no mercy."

"But you do." Lishen stared at him. "And it's a funny little coincidence, isn't it? You're going through your medicine faster too. When you were in the king's court, you informed the warden that you needed more. But you were restocked a month ago. Why are you taking so much more?"

"I was injured. I wasn't aware that there were rations on the medicine. I have been instructed to take it whenever the heat starts. Am I in error?"

"No. We wouldn't want you to die. But we are concerned about why you have suddenly had such a change in your requirements."

Corvin shrugged at this. "I got snagged in the boundary more than once. You know how powerful jellyfish venom is."

Lishen nodded. His expression unchanging, he struck Corvin with his fist, dropping him to the ground once more. "You made no mention of that in your report. Nor did you mention feeding the leviathans."

"There are already rumors about you, worm food," Black Claws sneered. He pushed the washbasin over. Water splattered all over the floor, the dishes inside shattering. The basin itself cracked.

"Rumors that have been addressed," Corvin growled. He stood once more, signaling Tagger to retreat again. "I have answered every inquiry on everything."

"All except...when did you feed the leviathans?" Lishen demanded.

Black Claws shoved the pot of stew onto the floor. The

broth and chunks of fish, potatoes, carrots, and tomatoes spilled out.

"After they destroyed the ship and I realized they were still hungry," Corvin said.

That was a lie.

I bit the inside of my lip, silently begging Lishen to believe his story and let him go.

"Well…we'll see, won't we?" Lishen said with a shrug. "But truly, there is one point that just keeps bothering me. It would seem that everyone but that pretty little female you claim drowned made it to the island," Lishen said, circling him. "And the funny thing is…the older woman—before the dwarf dragged her off—kept asking where her daughter was. She believes she's alive."

"Delusion, most likely," Corvin said flatly. "If she isn't on the island, then the girl is dead."

"Oh?" Lishen snickered. He crossed his arms. "That's the only other option?"

"What are you implying? I have no mate. I am not permitted, and I cannot take one," Corvin said sharply. "And if I could, I would not let her anywhere near you."

Lishen's nose wrinkled with disgust before he struck Corvin again. "You say that, but we both know what shifter fae do when they find their mates. It's practically uncontrollable. Nothing else matters. But it isn't like she had to be your mate for you to snatch her. You could have just grabbed her because you wanted something to warm your bed."

Corvin spat out a mouthful of blood and straightened his shoulders. "I have fire now."

The three fae laughed coldly. Then they attacked.

I cringed as the three fae beat Corvin, their blows falling swift and fierce. There were no more questions. Just strikes. The only thing that held me back was knowing I would make it worse for him if I revealed myself.

He staggered under the beating until he at last fell and did not stand. Blood dripped from his busted lip. His right eye swelled shut. The stripes along his face and body bulged and darkened in sickly shades.

Blue Ridges kicked Corvin onto his back. He then put his boot against his chest and seized Corvin's wrist with the claw bracelet. Corvin sputtered, choking on his own blood. Before he could do more than groan with pain, Blue Ridges snapped two of the claws in Corvin's bracelet directly into his wrist.

Corvin spasmed, the veins in his neck bulging. He gasped in agony.

Lishen pulled out the knife I'd used to chop the tomatoes. He held the blade up, looking it over. Then he jammed it in Corvin's side.

WOUNDED DARLING

I barely strangled my own cry of horror as the blade punched into Corvin.

No.

Corvin gave one strangled cry, his voice guttural. All the air had been driven from his lungs.

No, no, no!

Lishen seized a fistful of Corvin's hair and dragged him up to eye level. "This isn't over. We'll conduct our own investigations on this matter. Because the king is merciful, you will receive your medicine. But make no mistake, skin scraps, if we learn you have not been fulfilling the spirit and purpose of your duties, you will be punished. And if we find out you have a human—well…you know what will happen." He jerked his chin toward the door.

Blue Ridges snapped my wooden spoon and tossed it toward the woodstove. "More kindling for your fire." The pieces clattered on the metal top, one rolling toward the flame of the largest burner.

I set my jaw, my hands balling into fists.

Black Claws dragged the door open, waiting for Lishen to

go through. Lishen strode over the threshold. "You'll appear before the king in three days. Unless we find proof of your treachery before then." With that, he strode away. The other two followed, Black Claws pulling the door almost shut behind them.

Every fiber of my body screamed for me to run to Corvin right away.

But Corvin was shaking his head harshly, mouthing the word "no" over and over.

I froze. Even as the end of my cherished wooden spoon caught fire. Even as Corvin lay there motionless, his hand clasped over the serrated blade. His blood pooled on the stone floor, and he just kept mouthing the word "no."

Tagger wasn't moving from beneath the table. He too just stared at the door.

My entire body ached with the inaction.

The door slammed open again.

I almost let a startled scream slip out, my eyes bulging.

Black Claws stood there, scanning the room. He looked down at Corvin, eyes narrowing. "Pathetic," he growled. Then he spat on him. He jerked the door shut behind him.

This time the runes sealed over it.

As soon as the light of the runes flared and vanished, Tagger bounded to Corvin. He started nuzzling and licking him, whimpering and squeaking.

I shoved the panel back, practically falling out. The stone struck me hard, but I scrambled forward, barely feeling the pain. "Corvin!"

He dragged the blade out, his face contorting. His bright-green eyes had dulled, and the green and yellow of his flesh had faded to sickly hues. Dark veins sprouted around the two broken claws cutting into his wrists. His breathing was labored and shallow, his eyes glazed with pain. By the time I got up from my stumble, he was moving.

Limbs trembling, he struggled up on his knees and avoided the broken pottery and clay. His hand gripped the table, his claws digging into the wood as he drew in a ragged breath. He snatched the jar with his medicine and shoved a handful of the herbs straight into his bleeding mouth.

I grabbed the mildewed mats and dragged them back into the bedroom. The one blanket had been ripped in half, but it would still do for now. Though it was one of the saddest beds I'd ever seen, it was better than nothing.

I rushed to his side as he struggled forward. Though normally he towered over me, he leaned heavily against my shoulder as I helped him hobble to the makeshift bed. His breath came in shuddering gasps and his stripes continued fading to a sickly grey.

"Lie down." I eased him onto the mats.

"I just need to rest. I'll be fine," he said, his voice shaking at the end. He lay down on his side immediately. His tunic and trousers were soaked with blood.

"Do you need me to bind your wounds?"

"I've closed off the bleeding," he said weakly. "I'll be fine."

My heart pounded nonetheless. How could he survive all that?

"I didn't think they would come here," he murmured. "I—I was wrong. I was wrong, Mena."

"What can I do?" I placed my hand against his throat, checking his pulse. It was weak beneath my fingertips.

"I just—I just have to heal." His eyelids slid shut.

"You will." I stroked his silky hair, my fingers teasing at the curls. Why hadn't he defended himself? He'd taken the beating with little protest. And he'd protected Tagger and me. A knot of emotion formed in my throat, tears choking me. Those fae were just being cruel to him. "Do they often do this to you?"

He shook his head, his cheek resting against his arm as he

supported himself. "Worse this time. Lishen was angry. So was the king. I've made them suspicious."

"Do you want to talk about it?"

He shook his head.

I sat there with him in silence, watching and considering what had happened. He wasn't healing fast after that initial burst either. When I pressed him, he said it was just because of the internal wounds and the venom from two of the claws. "The venom is targeted at my blood as it is now to keep me in check. It's designed to be exceptionally painful and draining." His eyes remained shut.

More and more cruelty against him.

Had the bruising on his face gone down? Maybe a little. The deep cut across his lip had finally healed.

Tagger whimpered and nuzzled him. He then moved under Corvin's arm and put his wet snout directly on his chin.

I remained beside Corvin, feeling so helpless.

What could I do?

The air was thick and unpleasant with the odors of spilled stew, fresh blood, and charred wood. Though I hadn't asked a lot of questions in the shifter village, I had seen quite a bit. They had a medical facility attached to the tavern and the inn and the store. Shifters consumed huge quantities of food. They needed it for the energy. "Is it true that food and water helps? That you eat a lot to heal faster?"

He nodded, eyes firmly shut.

Well, that was something I could help with.

I halted when I saw the pieces of my spoon catching fire on the wood stove.

"No!" Lunging forward, I gripped the pieces of the wooden spoon and put out the flames licking along the end. I'd forgotten all about it until it was almost too late. It was going to be hard to repair.

"What's wrong?" Corvin called. He groaned as he started to get up. One of the wounds along his mouth and neck reopened. Blood trickled down his now-dull skin. He collapsed against the bed.

"Nothing, it's nothing. Don't worry about it," I said tightly. I pinched the bridge of my nose. It really wasn't worth his attention. There were far more important matters for us to worry about. Tears pricked my eyes as I set the broken pieces on the table. I didn't believe in dreams anyway.

Right now, I had to focus on the tasks at hand.

I went back into the storerooms and started searching for anything that might help strengthen his healing abilities.

Tagger remained by Corvin's side for about an hour before he padded out and disappeared. He returned with various fish and mollusks, piling them on the table.

I praised Tagger each time, and when he at last stopped, I scratched his chin and behind his ears. "You're very sweet. Just the very best," I said gently. He didn't chirp or squeak in response, and he rejected every treat I offered him until I returned one of the scallops to him. Even then he took it to Corvin and tried to make him eat it.

It took what felt like hours to clean up the destruction. There was another bin in the storeroom that I dragged out for all the broken pieces. There had to be glue somewhere in this place.

Maybe I could make some out of the fishbones? Maybe…

Taking care of Corvin was more important though, and right now, all I could really do to help him was ensure he had good nourishing food.

Thanks to Tagger's efforts, I now had haddock, mussels, shrimp, scallops, and small salmon. All fresh. All rich and flavorful.

Once I got the stew simmering, I cleaned up. It felt as if it took hours.

I discovered a splinter-riddled mop under one broken crate as well as a broom. No dust pan to be seen, so I made do with a broken bowl. Digging through the storeroom and searching revealed additional items. Even some white wine, which I promptly put into the stew. The tea tins I brought out along with a small pot would serve well enough to boil water and make some good tea.

Rifling through the items, I even found my mini-crossbow. Apparently Tagger had kept it. Incorrigible little beast.

Whenever I passed the little room where Corvin slept, I peeked in. Some of the wounds just didn't seem to be healing. He kept his hand over his side protectively. He had been able to heal me, even if he said it was an accident. So why was he struggling so much now?

Was it the venom?

How cruel was it that he had to live with venomous claws set against his wrist? Venom customized to his very blood. And he had to live here on top of all that.

Sometimes he trembled. Sweat beaded on his brow. He kept his jaws clenched tight.

I brought him water and made him a special tea I found in the storeroom as well. It smelled of green tea, ginger, lemon, and pomegranate. "Drink this," I murmured, hoping he would find my voice soothing. "I'll have food ready for you in a couple more hours."

He nodded tightly. "You don't have to do this," he said shakily.

"Just drink this."

He accepted it, his grip faltering a little on the mug.

"Do they often beat you this way?"

"When the mood seizes them."

"And you just take it?" I'd seen him shatter the ship like it was matchsticks. The other fae were strong as well, of course. But he could have done something. Or was he condemned to simply be their punching bag.

"So long as they don't hurt Tagger, I can manage. If you fight them too much, they just get meaner. And there's nowhere else for me to go. They can get fairly creative. This time they only had poison on their boot tips and claws."

"I didn't—I didn't even see those," I whispered.

"You're not supposed to see it. It's not deadly. Just painful." He stared at the wall, his eyes hooded. He swallowed hard. "Mena..."

"Yes?" I crouched beside him.

"If I asked you to swear to me that you would never leave me—even knowing all of this about me—would you swear it?"

My eyes widened. "What?"

It was a simple yet heavy question. One that should have been easy to answer at once.

Except for that look in his eyes. They pleaded for something—not a yes. But the desire.

And my hesitation—if that look was true, it cut him deeper than the blade Lishen stabbed in his side.

My heart shattered. "It isn't that—Corvin, I—"

"I don't want to talk anymore."

"Corvin," I started.

"It's all right," he said roughly, shaking his head. "It was stupid of me to think otherwise. I'll find a way to fix this. But I don't want to talk right now."

He refused to say much more, and chills came upon him again. Fever raged in his veins.

When the stew was finished, I fed it to him. He murmured his thanks, but he still refused to look at me. Almost as if he were ashamed.

Though I was exhausted, it was hard for me to rest. Even the slightest sound disturbed me.

Time was meaningless. I could estimate it roughly based on the fact that the broth in the stew kept cooking down, but it was hard to be precise.

In between my other tasks, I tried to make glue to mend my spoon. It didn't work, resulting in a sticky mess.

His healing was slow. I made him eat and drink every few hours, and I read from the book from my mama's desk. At least as much as I could. My thoughts often drifted to her.

Had Mama found the portal she was looking for? A way to reach the Oracle and find another clue in Erryn's disappearance? Mama was stranded on the island until the boundary moved and help came. Then she'd no doubt be back on her way to finding Erryn. She'd have to. She probably wouldn't leave that staircase as she searched for answers.

My heart twisted a little bit as I remembered the charge the fae had given: my mother was calling out for her daughter now.

But did Lishen mean Erryn or me?

Who would she choose if she had to?

Could there be a deeper hell to thrust anyone in than to choose between two people you loved?

I held my head and rocked back and forth, trying to calm the storm within me. Each time I drifted off, I startled awake soon after.

The only thing Corvin asked for was the medicine from the jar. He took it several times. Not once did he enjoy it, though he did enjoy the stew and tea I brought him. And though he refused to talk, as time passed, I noticed him watching me through hooded eyes, his gaze sad but hungry. It was clear he wrestled with something.

After all was cleaned up, I curled up beside him and put my arms around him. Just because he might be cold.

That was the only reason.

Wasn't it?

Yes.

Sweet night…

I hugged him, my chin pressed to his shoulder as I placed my hand over his.

Was he even awake?

His hand tightened over mine.

My heart pounded faster, my tongue thickening in my mouth. "Am I bothering you?"

"No. But I still don't want to talk. I need to think. Forgive me."

I squeezed his hand in response, then rested my cheek against his shoulder. He was a fair bit bigger than me. My being the big spoon was almost comical, but I wanted to comfort him. Even with all the questions that rose within me. Even knowing he was the reason I was down here. I just —I felt bad for him.

Tagger climbed up on us both and snuggled in. His tail flicked at Corvin's cheek before he tucked his tail around his hindquarters.

No trace of the striking cologne Corvin wore remained. We all smelled like fish, blood, must, and smoke. Yet it didn't make me want to pull away.

I just wanted him to feel better.

At last I fell asleep.

No dreams reached me.

When I woke, something felt changed. My eyes flew open.

Corvin and Tagger were gone.

CERTAIN

I sat up, fear surging through my veins. "Corvin? Tagger?" The blankets had been tucked around me, but they slid away as I jumped to my feet.

Even without the lack of response, I knew they were gone. The cavern felt empty without them, even with the stew simmering on the woodstove.

A piece of paper sat on the table under my spoon.

My spoon was fixed? The end was blackened from the flames, two of the runes burned away. But…he'd fixed it?

Somehow.

I picked up the paper then. It showed two stick figures and a small stick blob, one holding up a hand and the small stick blob, the other figure standing. Stay, maybe? Was the stick blob a hand? He and Tagger were going somewhere, but they'd be back?

I shook my head, dragging my fingers through my tangled hair. Worry flared within me. Not simply for Mama. Not just for me. For them.

Nothing had better happen to that stupid fae shifter or

his ridiculous otter. I clenched my fists, tears leaking down my cheeks.

Sniffling, I wiped my face and tried to find something to occupy my time. There was no way out right now. I almost thanked the Creator for that. Because that kept me from having to make a choice. A choice I should never have to make.

I belonged with Mama, taking care of her and making sure that she was all right. Even if I had been on the verge of telling her I'd had enough and we were going to settle down or I'd find my own path. And yet, thinking of leaving Corvin here—I pushed the thoughts away, my heart hammering.

He wasn't my mate. I was just a human.

I paced, examined the mini-crossbow, found the spare bolts in my pocket, and then made sure it was all in working order. Not that it would do much good here, but it soothed me to do something familiar.

I then read to distract myself, barely absorbing the words. He'd asked me to swear to stay. And I hadn't really answered him. He hadn't been angry either. Yet guilt rose within me.

What was wrong with me?

Why did it—why did the thought of leaving or wounding his feelings hurt?

The door scraped open. Tagger bolted in through the flap, not seeming to care that the door itself was already moving. Corvin followed close behind. His stripes still weren't their usual brightness.

I stood, my heart in my throat. "Where did you go?"

He stared at me, his hand on the door. "I'm ready to talk, Mena." He spoke the words with such calm and weight, but torment filled his eyes.

My stomach dropped. "Yes?" What did he want to talk about exactly? The entire mood had shifted between us. It was like standing on uneven ground.

He shut the door and strode closer. I was relieved to see he was steadier on his feet now. With a sigh, he dragged his fingers through his hair. "I went back to the island. This time I did speak with your mother."

"How is she?"

He opened his mouth to speak, then shook his head. "She's safe. And well. At least as well as one can be in her situation."

I stilled, staring at him, my hands folded tight against one another.

"I told her you were safe," he said. There was a heaviness in his voice, weighing down his shoulders. "I told her I hadn't harmed you. That I wouldn't. That I would…I would never." He covered his mouth, his head dropping. His mouth twitched. "I need to explain. When all this started, I didn't think your mother loved you."

I pulled back, frowning. "How could you say that?"

"Not all mothers love their children equally. My family abandoned me. As soon as it was known that I was diseased and I could never change from this…" He gestured toward his stripes, still not looking at me. "My own mother left me on the rocks to be found by the king's fae. And…well, you might not realize this, but even before our first encounter, I heard what was happening on the ship."

My eyes widened. "You mean the first time I saw you wasn't the first time you saw me?"

He shook his head. "I can travel all the neutral waters surrounding the North Sea, though I am not allowed to set foot on land. And as soon as the ship entered those waters, I heard your mother's wails for the daughter she had lost. I heard her conversations with Hosvir and all her thoughts and justifications. Plans from half-formed hopes and desperate acts to scrape together some clue about Erryn's location. I knew Erryn's name before yours. It took me three days to realize who you were to her. I didn't even know you were her daughter."

I flinched. "Don't…" I warned, my voice hoarse.

His brow lifted. "I'm not trying to wound you," he said. "I am only stating what I saw and how I felt. I—"

"I have watched my mother destroy her life searching for my little sister. But she loves me! I know she does."

He nodded then. "Yes. She does. You were the one who was supposed to stay and thrive. She leaned on you. You are the one who shouldered the impact of her grief along with your own sorrow. She sacrificed you—"

"I went willingly," I said, my voice sharpening despite the thick tears in my throat.

"It wasn't fair. You gave up everything, and she didn't even try to stop you."

"It's not her fault," I whispered.

But he was right.

I had given up everything. Suitors. Stability. Dreams. Home. There had been times I hated Mama and Erryn, but I'd also never stopped loving them. And it had always been my decision to keep going. They were my family. And I couldn't imagine staying behind. The fae who stole Erryn stole our lives as well, and I had no answers. It was only recently I had been coming to terms with the fact I had to do something different because this was bad for both Mama and me. "It isn't."

He dipped his head forward, his voice raspy. "Not all of it. You love her. I understand this better now. And she loves you, although that love has become twisted in her desperation to find your sister. Her love wasn't clear to me, but the rest of it was. And I—I thought I could save you."

I startled. This wasn't where I had expected the conversation to go.

"I wanted to rescue you," he continued. "I wanted you for

my own. I know—I know you aren't my mate. I'm forbidden to have one, and if I could have had a mate, the bond would have snapped into place between us almost at once. But still, I couldn't stay away from you. Especially when I heard—I heard so much."

"I didn't realize that anyone could hear us on the ship," I said, still struggling with this revelation.

"There are no secrets on the sea," he said, his gaze on the floor. "At least not many. Sound carries over the water." He raked his hand through his hair as he sat on the stool. It creaked and tipped forward until he braced his boot against the cracked stone. "Even before I saw you, I felt for you. And —I don't know fully what I was thinking. I thought—I thought I could give you something more, somehow...I wanted to take care of you. But I've brought you into such danger. And now you're the one taking care of me. My feelings for you got twisted, and it wasn't about what was best for you or even what you wanted."

I kept my arms crossed. Confusion knotted inside me. "I've just...I'm good at taking care of things."

"I know." His throat bobbed before he glanced up at me, a soft wetness in his eyes. "I wanted you to be mine. I wanted you to stay. But there's something I want more. I want to take care of you. And taking care of you means letting you go."

Those words hung in the air between us.

All I could do was stare.

"What are you saying, Corvin?"

"I am saying that I'm releasing you. I'll take you back. But I have to meet with the King of the North Sea. I can't slip out again without being spotted, and they will see me if I try to carry you through the waters."

My stomach clenched. I shook my head as I remembered

the three fae who had come here. "They're going to hurt you, aren't they?"

He shrugged, his manner heavy and subdued. His claws pressed against his temples. "They have questions. They'll likely harvest my blood."

"Harvest your blood?" Alarm flared through me. How could his situation get worse every time we spoke? I suddenly recalled what Hosvir had said.

He nodded. "All the shifter fae are required to provide blood. It's early this time, but when we shifter fae have erred in the past, the king has required a heavier blood tithe. They have no other evidence of my violating the laws. Once they've taken what the king requires and satisfied themselves, they'll stop. Then they'll get off my back, and they won't be watching this place so closely. When I return, I'll take you back to your mother. In case something goes wrong, I've told Tagger to stay here with you. If I don't come back, he'll guide you through the water. Just tell him to take you to the Kabroks."

I bit the inside of my lip, tears pricking my eyes. He meant it. He actually meant it. And everything was becoming clearer. Including the thoughts I pondered in the past days. "It was just the ship, wasn't it?"

He grunted. "What?"

"You said over and over that the ship had to be destroyed."

He twitched his shoulder, but his gaze dropped.

"And you did know Captain Hosvir. It's why you came to see the ship. You knew it. There was a meeting place on the island. It's why he was willing to risk the boundary to get my mother where she wanted to be. He knew—he knew you were looking for the loophole too. And it's why the crew all cooperated." I shook my head. "I figured they weren't fighting you on the ship because they were too terrified. But no... They knew who you were. It's why they cooperated so fast."

"The law is merciless. And it was fulfilled to the letter."

"You don't want to be an enforcer."

He shook his head, his lips pressed in a tight line. One thin split still ran the length of his lip and chin, a trace of the abuse from the earlier day. "It was that or die from starvation or exposure or the disease that makes me this way. And I took the vow to serve the king so long as I remained in his territory when I was ten. It was my choice. Just as it has been my choice to fulfill only the letter of his law rather than its spirit."

"Why didn't you tell me?" I whispered.

"There are no secrets above the sea. Places like this are safe. But you never know who is listening above or in the open water. And once you were here with me, I started to realize it was a mistake. A mistake I can't even understand why I made." He bowed his head, the following words agonizing. "Shifter fae like me—we just don't have mates. Yet —" He looked at me, his eyes hooding. His breath caught in his throat. "I can't explain it. Every time I look at you, Mena, all I feel is hunger and need. I wasn't sure what it was at first. I—I'd never felt it before. It isn't as if I haven't flirted or even traded kisses or affection. But it never meant anything. It never awoke anything except a desire to see others flustered or off balance." He shrugged and let his arm fall to his side. "But with you...from the moment I saw you, all I have realized is what I lack."

Something inside me splintered. I moistened my lips and squared my shoulders. "So why did you want me to come with you down here? Was it just to save me from what you thought was a mother who didn't care about me?" I asked, my voice choked. "If you can't have a mate—"

"No. It just slipped out the first time. The invitation. And then the idea behind it grew. The thought of no longer being alone. The thought of being near you. I wanted—" He shook his head. "What I wanted was unfair. Especially now when I realize the kind of person you are. You take care of people. And no one takes care of you. I wanted to take care of you, but I'm too broken to know how to do that as well as I would like. I think maybe people like you are rivers that give until they are dry. Then they mourn, not because they are empty but because they wish so much that they had more to give. And I have to let you go or you will die in this place."

His words both cut and comforted me. "Corvin—" I started.

He stepped closer and took my hands in his. His claws lightly scraped my skin. "I thought I could hide you here. I didn't think they would notice that you were missing from the ship. I didn't think..." He bowed his head. "Cruel as they were to me, they would be worse to you. I know now I can't protect you. And this place is wretched." He pressed his fore-head to mine. "I am so sorry, Mena."

My breaths grew ragged. "What makes you so certain I'm not your mate?" I whispered, my voice shaking. That rational part of my mind told me this was fast, and yet...it did not feel wrong. "I understand—I think—that there's a disease. But what if that's wrong? What makes you so certain?"

"The mate bond hasn't come together," he whispered. "It's simple."

"How do you know?"

"It would change me. And you. It would change me at my core. In my muscles. My blood. My very life."

"Is that why you kept grabbing my ankle and trying to touch me?"

He shrugged slightly and managed a smile. The corners faltered. "When I first saw you and caught your scent, some-thing stirred in me. I hoped..." He swallowed hard, then nuzzled me. His eyes shuttered. "You are not my mate, Mena. But if I could choose one, I would choose you. I tried to choose you, but I can't condemn you to this fate." His breath wisped against my cheek. "I can't keep you here. I was wrong to tear you away as I did."

"We made a bargain," I protested, my voice hoarse. "I agreed to come with you."

"I was going to save everyone I could on your ship anyway. I manipulated you into coming with me." His fingertips stroked my cheek before he stepped back. He paced across the room, sighing. "You're always going to give. And if I am to…care about you, then I must care for you as you are. Pretending that you would be anything but yourself was cruel of me. And I'm sorry, Mena. For everything. I want to make you happy, but I have no idea how to do it. Especially not in a wretched place like this. All the warmth and goodness here is because of you. All I've done is drag you into torment and suffering. And words will never fully express how much I regret that. How much it breaks my heart to even think of you being hurt because of it. But that night on the ship when you chased after me…"

I cut my gaze up at him as I folded my arms. "What about that night?" My heart beat faster now, emotion choking me.

His gaze raked over me. I wasn't nearly so well put together now as I had been then. My hair was frizzy, my clothing mussed, wrinkled, and smelling of the sea. But he looked at me as if he saw beneath all of that and craved every inch of me. My whole body tensed.

"Well?" I demanded, my breaths ragged now. He'd looked at me so many times, heating my blood. But now—now it was as if everything had lit up within him.

No one would ever look at me like he did.

And I was terrified and aroused at once.

Not simply because of him, but because of me.

He crossed toward me, backing me against the wall once more. His hand struck the rocky surface, caging me in and setting my pulse raging. Then he leaned closer, his nose grazing mine.

I swallowed hard, my core tensing and heat pooling in my belly. But I waited—waited to see what he was going to do.

His breath whispered against my lips.

"I don't understand it," he said. "What I feel for you when I look at you...when I hold you—" He let out a low, rumbling growl that made me gasp. "There are things I want to do to you. Things that aren't supposed to be possible. Things I shouldn't."

I held my breath. "Why not?"

"You're not my mate," he said hoarsely, the words sounding painful to him. "I should never have taken you. I can't make you mine, no matter how much I want you. And I need to get you out of here. I have to get you somewhere safe."

His tongue pressed at his lips as he wet them. He leaned a little closer, the heat from his body reaching me.

I stared up at him, eyes wide. His body had felt so good pressed against mine during the past nights. Now I ached to feel the whole of him against me, crushing me into the wall and exploring every line, every curve.

His thumb grazed my temple as his other hand slipped to my throat. His fingers pressed against my skin, the tips of his claws making my skin pebble as delicious shivers rushed through me.

Kiss me.

Kiss me now.

My lips parted as he stroked a line from my ear to my jaw. He started to pull back.

"Come with me," I whispered.

He tilted his head, his eyebrow flicking up.

"You and Tagger, we'll all run away. We'll get my mother and everyone else on the island, and we'll get away from here. Get you out of the king's power. I won't leave you. You'll leave with me."

His smile pulled crooked, but that sad hunger remained in his eyes. "If only I could."

"Why can't you? We may not be mates, but—"

He removed his hand from my throat and showed me his wrist. The two claws from the bracelet were still embedded in his skin; the flesh was swollen around them.

Several remained.

"At the king's command, these claws will puncture my wrist, injecting me with venom. He doesn't have to be close to me to do it. It is enough for him to utter the command, and they will inject one at a time, leading to a tortuous death. Or at least paralysis and helplessness while his faithful servants drag me back. There's no escape for me, clever girl. The venom has been made specifically for me to attack my blood and my body."

I shook my head. There had to be another way. Tears rolled down my cheeks.

His clawed finger slipped beneath my chin and tilted my face up to his. "What's this? Are you really crying for me? So soon? After all I've done? You really are a priceless treasure, darling."

"I don't understand why I'm feeling so much so fast, but… the thought of leaving you here in this place—you and Tagger both—I can't." I scrunched my eyelids shut for a breath. This was happening so quickly, and it made no sense. But it burned so true.

"If I could, I'd be there with you in my arms or on my knees asking for you to be mine. Fate and king be damned." He nudged me with his nose. The low rumbling groan that pulled from his lips almost undid me. "The only thing I want right now is to know you have a chance to live. Really live, Mena."

"And that doesn't extend to you? Don't you deserve to live?"

"Fate and life aren't about what's deserved. Simply what is." He pressed his finger to my lips. "You have a chance, Mena. I'm going to make sure you get it. I just ask that you think about what you want for your life and don't always think immediately about what others want or need."

"And what if what I want is for you to kiss me?" I whispered.

His breath hitched. He licked his lips again. "If I start to kiss you, I won't stop. I'll kiss you until you're breathless and shaking and the only reason you're still standing is because I'm holding you up."

"And you would deny me that?"

His eyes widened as his hand flattened against the wall by my head. His other hand curled into my hair, tipping my head back as he leaned in—

Heavy fists beat on the door.

INTRUDERS

I started to curse, but Corvin clamped his hand over my mouth. He leaned against me, his breaths ragged. "Stay quiet." His claws dug into my cheek momentarily. "I have to deal with this. They'll torture and kill you if they find you."

My nerves still frayed and raging, I nodded.

He hefted me into the smuggler's space behind the bookshelf again and pulled the panel shut. Then he crossed to the door.

The fae who stood on the other side was all silver-scaled with diamond-shaped eyes. Several others stood behind her. "The King of the North Sea demands your attendance immediately."

Corvin released a tight breath. "I am aware of my summons. I have—"

"You will come now. Your blood is required."

Sighing, Corvin leaned against the door frame. "Just let me have the next two hours. The venom from the claws has left me weakened. My blood will be stronger and of more use if I am allowed the rest."

"The king's orders are the king's orders," the fae said, her voice cold as the waters she'd come from. "I have been instructed to bring you into his presence. Your blood is required immediately."

He sighed, then straightened. He pushed his thick black curls out of his striped face. "Let me make sure Tagger has his instructions. I don't want him running off again."

Tagger stood near the bookshelf, tense as a bowstring. He cocked his head and squeaked as Corvin approached. Corvin crouched and stroked him.

"I suppose this is sooner than I thought and rather unexpected. But I will only be gone for a little bit," Corvin said, far louder than usual. "But if I do not return within a day or so, you are free to leave, to hunt and swim and follow the paths to whatever places you wish. Take a friend to the Kabroks. Hmmm? Look after each other. Stay alert. You won't be alone for long."

I pressed my face to my forearm, forcing back a sob.

They were going to punish him. Hurt him.

They were going to torture him for not killing everyone on the ship.

"You think that otter can understand you?" the fae guard scoffed. She snapped her fingers and pointed toward the doorway. "Go. Sooner you answer, sooner you can return." She gave him a nasty shove. As he staggered forward, she pressed something into the lock with her long silver claw.

My eyes widened. Salt's bane, I hated this fae guard as much as the fae warriors who had attacked him. They were coming back, weren't they?

As the door clicked shut, I scrambled down and pulled the panel shut. I hurried to the door and pulled it open with ease. Despite the clicking sound, the door wasn't locking. I tried to pry the silver out, but I only loosened a bit of it.

Not good enough.

And dangerous.

If those goons returned, I had to make sure there was no trace of me here. Tagger squeaked, trailing after me as I ran to the door.

"If I find a way to block it, they're going to know I'm in here," I said, pushing my hair out of my face. And I wasn't strong enough to remove that bit of silver. Whatever I did couldn't be something that would make it easier for them to convict and torture Corvin.

Tagger offered a series of trills as he hopped up on the stool. It tilted to the side, almost sending him reeling.

Think. Think, think. Think!

I grabbed the mini-crossbow from the counter and then pulled out the blue-tipped bolts. Two of them were in good enough condition to use again. The other two had been damaged in the struggles and swim. If I made my own sedative or poison, they could be useful.

I then stoked the fire and filled the stew pot almost to the brim with water so that it wouldn't burn.

I had a bad feeling about this. If Lishen and his fae came back, they would be searching for proof of my existence and who knew what else to condemn Corvin. The bookshelf was tricky to get into without Corvin there to help me, but they had missed it already.

Uncomfortable as it would be, this was where I would stay. I gathered up some supplies for myself, including one of the butcher knives, a little ball, my spoon, my flint, and a waterskin. Before I climbed inside, I fixed the bolt into the mini-crossbow. Hopefully it wouldn't be necessary. I started to climb in, then stopped.

Should I bring Tagger with me?

The otter stood by the bookshelf, staring up at me with his snout wriggling.

I couldn't risk leaving him out here.

It was just a feeling, but the last time one of the fae had tried to kick him. "Come on, sweet baby." I scooped him up as I would a toddler, his paws resting on my shoulder. I climbed up the shelf and slid inside. "You're going to have to be so quiet," I whispered. He was a smart boy. Surely he understood.

Once I was safely situated behind the hidden panel, I drew it mostly shut. There was just enough light for me to read. And this little book might now hold a way for us to get out of here together.

Tagger sniffed at me and chewed on the ball. He then nuzzled me, asking for scratches.

I obliged.

Time passed slowly. Tagger's soft, huffing breaths were almost masked by the crackling of the fire.

I pored over the pages of Mama's book, my heart hammering as I searched for answers. Her tidy handwriting, even blurred from the sea, held many secrets and theories regarding the portals and staircases. I wasn't certain what had made Mama obsess on these particular ones months ago. But—this could work.

Soon, I'd be able to ask her. I'd ask her and thank her. Yes. I could imagine hugging Mama again. I could practically imagine the arguments sure to ensue when I told Mama that I wanted to be with Corvin. And oh—they would be good arguments. Tears blurred my vision, and I forced myself to focus on the pages. I'd tell Corvin all about this when he got back. And we'd run away.

Some of the notes were hard to read, but several points confirmed what I remembered: the portals summoned at the top of the grounded staircases could be managed, unlike the wild staircases which appeared and disappeared without a trace. They were actual holes that opened up into reality.

One could escape any boundary or restriction thanks to these portals.

And there was that temple close to here—the remnant from the one on the island, a temple lost in the sea or perhaps built inside a mountain in the sea—perhaps built into the same stone that this cave was in. If we got to it, we could see if the portal responded. If it had enough strength left and the staircase its magic reached was likewise prepared, then we could escape through it.

Tagger snuffled.

I stroked his head. "We're going to figure this out. We'll fix it. Together."

The door slammed open. I clenched, curling tight around Tagger. It took all my presence of mind to slide the panel fully shut once more.

Lishen strode in. "Come out! If you're hiding, human, come out, and we'll show you mercy."

Blue Ridges and Black Claws followed behind, searching the area with calculating gazes.

I closed my eyes and released a tight breath. Tagger wriggled.

The three began wrecking the place. They were even more thorough this time than before. Any place that they could see that was large enough to hold a human, they opened and tossed all the items onto the floor. Books, pottery, trinkets. One of the pale-blue orbs dropped from its iron holder and shattered, emitting an unpleasant lightning-like scent.

Blue Ridges came to the bookshelf where I hid. He raked his arm across the shelf, knocking out the pieces.

I held my breath.

Tagger pressed hard against me, miraculously staying quiet. Such a good, smart boy. He did understand.

JESSICA M. BUTLER

"If he does have a human in here, he's hidden her well," Black Claws growled. "Maybe he put her outside in the cave."

"He wouldn't do that. Too dangerous. He's a shifter fae. They're primal. When it comes to their mates, even before the mate bond goes into place, they get obsessive and irrational."

I tensed. They were referring to me as his mate as if it were an obvious fact. Was it just an assumption? Or did they know something else?

"If he has anyone here at all," Black Claws grumbled. He turned over one of the cupboards. The top cracked in a jagged split.

"He's got someone," Lishen responded. "It's the only thing that explains how fast he's burning through it and everything else. It's treason. Keep looking. Look for anything. Any proof."

"Why doesn't the king just execute him if he's so convinced?" Black Claws demanded. He shoved over the stool, then kicked open the guest bedroom again. Blue Ridges had gone into the storeroom. From the rustle and clatter and shattering that came from inside, he was doing a great deal of damage.

Lishen turned on Black Claws and seized him by the tunic, his eyes flashing with rage.

"The king wants proof first. Evidence that Corvin has betrayed us by harboring a human."

Black Claws scoffed, but his voice shook. "So the king needs proof of something he already believes? Seems foolish. You know he's guilty, Lishen."

"Perhaps. That doesn't change the need for proof. The king likes his fun. These charges are no fun without proof," Lishen growled.

The fae ransacked the cave, overturning furniture and smashing anything they deemed suspicious. I huddled in the hidden nook, heart pounding, willing Tagger to stay silent. He burrowed against me, his dark-purple eyes glittering through the thin slice of light that pierced our hiding place. I held my finger to my lips.

Not a sound, baby.

He tucked his head against my arm.

It seemed to go on forever, the two fae ruthlessly searching every inch of the cottage. Finally Lishen spoke again, his voice tight with frustration. "There's nothing here. No sign of any human. Not even another female." He spat a curse.

"I told you," growled Black Claws.

"Silence!" Lishen snapped.

Black Claws cringed and then bolted out of the room as the larger fae lifted his armored hand.

Blue Ridges chuckled darkly. "I'm going to hang back here. That otter'll come back soon. Asha said he commanded it to remain. It probably just went fishing. I'll gut it and string it up. Good lesson for the flesh scraps about what happens when he considers disobeying the king."

I hugged Tagger tighter. The otter wriggled in my arms, but he remained silent, poking my neck with his nose and whispers.

Please don't make a sound, baby. I closed my eyes and pressed my head to his.

Lishen gave a careless wave of his hand. "Do as you wish. But do not delay in returning. If the king gives the word, the hunt begins in a matter of hours. The skin scraps will be good for a chase, even if his mate dies fast."

"It won't take that long." Blue Ridges closed the door behind Lishen. He then strode over to the stool and sat down facing the door, as if he expected Tagger to return at any minute.

Rage burned within me. Over the years, I had met so

many despicable people. And this waste of fae magic was one of the worst. I picked up the mini-crossbow and checked the bolt. Good. Perfectly in place. He'd have one hell of a headache when he woke.

I slid the panel back slowly. The stew continued to bubble and simmer on the stove, the lid rattling occasionally as the logs hissed and popped.

Blue Ridges continued to stare at the door, ready to pounce when Tagger returned.

My upper lip curled as I took aim.

Then, easy as breathing, I squeezed the trigger. The tranquilizer struck him dead in the back of the neck.

With a half-uttered curse, he grabbed at his neck and slumped.

I rolled out of the hiding place and struck the ground feet first.

Tagger leaped down and chittered. "That's right, Tagger," I said, setting the crossbow aside, rage like ice in my heart. "We're going to conduct our own interrogation."

ANSWERS FOR ME

*I*t didn't take long to bind Blue Ridges. I put him in one of the chairs and lashed him to it with prickly ropes from the storeroom, not taking any care to be gentle. He'd be down for maybe another five minutes or so if I did nothing. And that was all I needed.

It was high time I got answers.

Tagger stayed closer to me, sniffing at the broken pottery as I made my preparations.

I set the butcher knife on one of the upright counters and the mini-crossbow on another. I plucked the bolt from his neck. It left a bloody mark. Apparently he didn't have self-healing like Corvin.

Good. That made it easier for me.

Next I checked the door. That bit of silver the fae had pushed in with her claw had fallen out now, so the lock worked again.

A little favor on our side, at least. I kicked the silver out into the water, then went back inside and secured his ropes, hoping it hurt when he woke.

This wasn't going to be pretty, but I didn't care. All that mattered was getting answers.

I crossed back in front of Blue Ridges.

Still unconscious.

I picked up the cracked pitcher, dunked it in the well, and brought it back over to him. Water streamed from the cracks. With a grunt, I flung it at him. The water crashed over his face.

He gasped, surging awake. The ropes kept his wrists and ankles bound. Though he panted, he remained groggy. "What?"

I remained silent, watching him, my expression steeled. Already my stomach twisted, but I wasn't going to back down. "You're going to answer my questions," I said coldly.

He looked up, water dripping from his face and hair. His eyes narrowed as soon as he saw me. "I knew it," he growled. "I knew you were here."

"Except you didn't find me. You and your friends aren't as good as you think."

Blue Ridges licked his bloodied lip, his gaze narrowing. "Doesn't matter. You'll be found. And then the fun will start."

"What kind of fun?"

"If you knew half of what was going to happen to you, you'd be wailing and begging for mercy."

"Oh? You aren't going to offer to help me if I let you go or don't harm you?" I folded my arms as I stepped back, examining him. Blue Ridges had more bulk than Corvin, and he moved slower. But if he got loose, I'd have to stop him fast. His hands were calloused and muscled, as were his arms.

I straightened my shoulders. No. If he got free, I'd have to kill him. Fast.

Blue Ridges spat at me. The bloody spittle struck the ground near my foot. "There is no mercy for the flesh scraps's mate."

My eyebrow raised. "Why is his mate such an important thing? And why do you call me that?"

"Why else would he be trying to protect you?" he snarled.

"It gets lonely down here, I'd imagine," I responded, voice flat. I paced, keeping my steps slow and deliberate. I'd never conducted an interrogation like this alone before, but I'd seen it done. I kept myself from blinking as I stared him dead in the eye, even though my eyes burned. "Why would it matter?"

Blue Ridges spat at me again as he struggled against the ropes. "Bite me, whore. You don't have the guts to kill me. And even if I don't get free, they'll notice when I don't return, and they'll come to the last place I was. Right here. You've courted yourself a big batch of trouble."

I picked up the knife and brandished it in front of his face. "Don't bother trying to escape," I said. "Those knots could hold a bear. And I want answers."

Blue Ridges glared at me, his strange eyes filled with hatred. "You'll pay for this in blood."

"If by blood, you mean your blood, yes, I will. If you don't cooperate with me and answer all my questions, I will make your stay here very unpleasant."

He spat at me again. This time his bloody spittle caught the edge of my boot. "You don't have it in you."

"You know, it's funny. People look at me, and they think they know me. If they notice me at all. But they never really see me, and they never guess what I'm actually capable of. You're not different in that respect. But I assure you, I can and will make you talk." To prove my point, I slid the blade across the top of his hand.

Blue Ridges yelped, then gritted his teeth as blood welled from the shallow cut.

"What difference does it make if Corvin has a mate? And why would it be forbidden when there is a disease that keeps him from having one? You all seemed very upset at the thought he might have a human here and made a lot of assumptions."

Blue Ridges shook his head.

I dragged the blade over his arm again.

He howled, struggling against the ropes and swearing at me.

"If you'd rather, I can start on your fingernails," I snarled. "Or I can go get salt water."

"What in the abyss are you?"

"I'm a woman who has had more than enough," I growled at him. "Now answer my questions! I don't give a damn if you bleed out in here. By the time your friends realize you're missing, I'll be long gone. And I don't give two fishbones whether you live."

He stared at me, his upper lip curling. Blood dripped from the cuts.

I sliced the blade over his arm again. "Answer me!"

He howled.

"Answer me, or I will start chopping off body parts. And I don't know what part I'm starting with."

"Fine, fine!" He stared at me with wide eyes, sweat pouring off his brow. "It doesn't matter anyway. You're dead."

"Amazing all the damage I can do despite being dead," I said, my voice low. I stepped closer, lifting the knife.

"Shifter fae with mates aren't as good at protecting the king's interests. Their blood is more potent when they are unmated and forced to have a single shifted form with their human form," he shouted. His breaths were ragged, his eyes white-rimmed. "If they're mated, they're distracted. Their focus is on their mates. They put their strength into protecting their families. Single, unattached shifter fae are the best enforcers and guardians because all that matters is what they are ordered."

"So this king condemns them to a life of loneliness and servitude?"

"It's necessary for the protection of the kingdom," he said, panting. "Shifter fae are worth less than regular fae anyway. They're little more than animals with quirks. Not much better than humans except when used as expendables in high-risk situations like enforcers. This is the only way shifter fae are valuable to the king."

I mulled this over. "So the disease isn't real?"

He scoffed. "The shifter fae are the disease. Do you know how many wars those horny bastards have caused? No, you wouldn't, cause you're a know-nothing human. But don't worry. The king will have you both dragged to the hunt. He'll have made accommodations to ensure you can suffer before you die. You'll die before your mate. They'll make sure of it. Losing their mate is the worst pain a shifter fae can experience."

"And there are other shifter fae like Corvin?" I studied him. He was being much more cooperative now. And he no longer seemed to be struggling. What was he planning? He didn't seem afraid of me gaining this knowledge, so clearly he intended to kill me.

"Over half the enforcers are like your waste-of-space mate, and all the shifter fae are diseased." He let out a rasping laugh, though the sound was forced. "They're dangerous, and having mates makes them unpredictable. The king keeps them isolated and mateless to maintain order. Their only calling is to do his will, and their blood is at its most powerful for alchemical combinations when unmated."

"His magic has no hold past the boundaries of his land, though," I confirmed, pacing.

"You think you can run away with your mate and find some form of happiness out there?" He laughed, his voice harsh. "Well, sure, if you can get past the hunt and the

163

boundaries. This whole sea will be churning with predators searching for the both of you. And even if you figured out some way to escape the deep without drowning, there are still the claws in your mate's arm."

Right. Those damnable claws! "What can be done to counter the venom?"

He scoffed. "You think I know that? What do you think I am, human?" He spat at me again.

I grimaced, wrinkling my nose at him. Disgusting. I slashed the blade over his arm again.

He yelped, struggling harder as he glared at me.

"What do you know about it?" All his words rolled over me. It felt as if I struggled to take them onboard, but I couldn't stop and process them.

He snarled. "The venom is made specifically for each enforcer. No antidote either."

"And the medicine they give Corvin...it's making it worse, isn't it?" I set my jaw. The rage boiled inside me.

"Only way to keep them from finding their mates and in the right headspace. Makes them strong where it counts. You should never have come here or talked to him."

"Yeah, I'm sure you'd prefer it that way."

"You shouldn't be so smug. You aren't the first mate to get through to an enforcer. All that means is there's got to be a spectacle. An example has to be made of both of you." Blue Ridges sneered. "Which is why you won't make it if you take to open waters, you pathetic waste of flesh. At best, you'll die down here alone. Or they'll come back here and find you eventually. Do you really think the king just sent for the shifter fae to have a nice little chat?"

I paused. "What do you mean?"

"Do you really think the king will let him go? He's as good as dead now. And whether someone's found you to drag you in, he'll be drained of more blood and then dropped into the hunt. Even if he escapes that, the king will start setting off those claws until he's all but paralyzed. Then we'll find him. Best way would be if he almost escaped and survived and *then* we found you so we could tear you apart in front of him. Regardless of how it goes though, your beloved will be praying for death before the sun sets."

I had to warn him.

No. It was too late for that.

What was I supposed to do? My mind spun. Could I send a message? How?

Every possibility I came up with was either impossible or unusable. I dragged my hand through my hair.

Wood crunched. Something snapped.

Tagger shrieked.

I spun.

Blue Ridges had broken the chair and now charged me, teeth bared, eyes hard.

I brought the butcher knife down, but he caught me on the downswing.

His hand clamped cruelly around my wrist as he slammed me into the wall.

Light exploded in front of my eyes. I couldn't even get out a gasping breath.

He clenched his hands around my throat as the knife dropped from my fingers. "The king will flay you alive and feed you to his pets. They'll cut your flesh and grind your bones down for potions and charms, but no one will care if I break a few before I drag you there." His thumbs crushed against my windpipe as he pinned me there.

Dark spots danced before my eyes.

DECLARATION

*lue Ridges used his weight to pin me to the wall,
his fingers crushing along my throat. I flailed at
the side of his head and clawed at his face, but he just
laughed.

"You'll suffer so much before you die," he gloated.

Tagger bit him in the back of the calf.

With a grunt, Blue Ridges kicked him viciously.

"Don't hurt him!" I barely managed to choke the words
out as I struck at Blue Ridges.

Cursing, he backhanded me, and my head struck the wall.
Blood filled my mouth. Everything slowed.

Blue Ridges flung me across the room. My body cracked
against the stone as he pounced on me again. "Don't worry,
you pathetic little human." He kicked me in the side. "I won't
kill you. I'll just kill the otter. Then I'll reunite you with your
love. You'll have so much fun." He kicked me again and again,
laughing.

I grabbed for the knife but grasped my stew spoon
instead. I cracked it across his face. The glue bond snapped,
and the pieces fell apart.

Blue Ridges cuffed me. I staggered backward, striking one of the stools. I met the ground.

Snarling, he leapt on me.

The force of his weight on me drove the air from my lungs. His fingers clamped around my throat. The taste of my own blood filled my mouth.

Everything blurred.

I jammed the broken end of the spoon into his shoulder near the juncture of his neck.

He recoiled, screaming, then hit me again. A knife flashed in his hand as he lifted it over me.

The door slammed open.

"Don't you dare touch her!" an animalistic voice bellowed. A great streaked shape lunged at him, tackling him to the ground.

"Corvin?" I struggled to open my eyes. Even breathing hurt.

Corvin seized Blue Ridges by the throat and slammed his head back again, rendering him unconscious or killing him. I couldn't tell. "You hurt her, you deal with me," he snarled.

"Corvin!" His name stumbled out of my mouth, slurred.

His gaze snapped up to me, his expression nearly feral.

Before I could say his name again, he grabbed me. He pressed his bloodied hand against the back of my head, tangling his fingers in my hair and cradling me to his chest. His breaths whooshed against my neck.

"I'm fine." I tried to pull my mind back into focus. My heart hammered, and my head spun. Pressing my cheek to his shoulder, I tried to ground myself.

He was back.

Corvin.

He was all right.

My eyelids slid shut, breathing in his scent. Like Tagger, he now smelled more like fish and salt, but I didn't care. It was him. "They were going to kill you. The king." My voice rasped.

"That's not important." He held me close. His cheek pressed against mine. Golden light flashed between us. He stiffened, not letting me go.

"No—" I bristled, pushing back. "What do you mean that's not important? The king is going to take all your blood. He's going to kill you." I paused, realizing the pain in my throat and sides had vanished. Some minor soreness and weariness remained, but nothing serious. "You didn't use medicine..."

His bright-green eyes remained wide as he traced his claw down my throat from where a bruise had been to my bloodied hand. The blood remained, but not the cuts and scrapes. His thumb stroked along the back of my hand. "No... I didn't." He frowned as he turned my wrist over. Some of the bruising remained. "You started to heal..."

Was he injured? The vivid colors had returned to his stripes and face, but there were scrapes and scars.

"I'm healed enough." I placed my hand on his chest, staring up into his eyes. "Corvin..."

He was looking at me strangely now, his hand flattening over my throat. "I healed you...again..." He curled his claws lightly against my skin, his gaze fixed upon me with something like reverence and awe.

My breath caught in my throat.

He knew.

And so did I.

His throat bobbed as his claws lightly traced a line up to my lips as he held me close. "How can you be so beautiful? So perfect?" he whispered.

Tears spilled down my cheeks. Looking up into his eyes, I felt—I wasn't just seen. I was seen and accepted and wanted.

He leaned down and nuzzled me. A trembling breath escaped me.

His lips brushed mine, featherlight.

Something stirred in me, heating with each breath and flaring through me.

A low growl rumbled from his chest as his tongue pressed against my lips.

That set my pulse surging and thundering.

With a moan, I returned his kiss.

The moment that moan escaped me, his arms tightened around me. He engulfed me as I clung tight. My fingers tangled in his hair.

Salt's bane, this fae could kiss! That rumbling purr that vibrated through his chest drove me wild. I needed to be close to him.

I had to be closer!

"Mine," he growled against my mouth.

Before I could repeat it, his mouth devoured mine.

My hands rubbed along the contours of his shoulders and up the back of his neck before curling once again in his silky-soft hair. Sharp jolts of pleasure shot through me as I rubbed against him. I loved him. He was mine, and I was his.

I knew what I wanted.

I wanted him.

"My sweet mate," he gasped. The sound grew ragged as his eyelids shuttered, and he held me tighter, his forehead pressing to mine. "And I have to let you go." His voice shook at the end, racked with pain.

His words cut through me. I froze.

No.

No!

I wasn't going to lose him.

"Come with me," I said hoarsely. My fingers pressed against his scalp and neck as I clung to him. "You and Tagger. Come with me. We'll find a way. We'll get you away from the King of the North Sea. We'll get you away from all of this."

He dipped his head forward. A shudder passed through him as he held me closer. "I don't know how this happened. I don't understand it. But, darling, you are the most precious gift in my life, and I can't let them destroy you."

"Listen to me." I bit back a sob. "Just listen to me, Corvin. You have to come with me. They've been lying to you all your life. Those herbs *are* suppressants. They've blocked you from finding your mate and shifting. You aren't diseased. They're using you and the other shifter fae. Harvesting your blood. Keeping you isolated. You started burning through the medicine after we met because…"

He pressed his finger to my lips, his bright eyes soft now. "All my life," he whispered, his voice rough and resonant with emotion. "All my life I have been alone. I thought I would always be alone. I had no mate, yet I longed for one. And now it turns out there was someone for me. Even better, she's the one I would have picked if I could."

I knew what I felt. It was intoxicating, powerful, and comforting all at once. "So you do feel the bond? That's what this is?" I wanted to stay in his arms forever. To never be apart from him. It all made sense.

He nodded as he nuzzled me, but sadness filled his voice. "The mate bond is coming into place. It's working in my blood and my core even now. But, my dear sweet, beautiful Mena, it doesn't matter. It's more important than ever that I get you to safety. The only comfort that will be left to me is knowing you are alive and safe."

"Why can't you come with me? If you get onto the island, we'll protect you. I'll fight to the death to protect you!"

"The magic prevents me from setting foot on the island of my own will. Even if you dragged me onto the land, it would pull me back eventually." He shrugged. "The best I'll be able to do is get you back to your mother. Hosvir has already alerted Baider. Another ship is on its way. The boundary line will shift again, and they will be able to rescue you. Now come on. Once the king discovers my treachery, he'll start activating the claws in my wrist. If I'm in the water when that happens, it will make me far easier to track."

"Then we'll find some other way," I said sharply. "I'm not leaving you behind. What about the temple with the staircase and the portal?" I ripped out the book from my pocket and opened it to one of Mama's drawings. "The one whose twin is on that island."

He scowled. "It would still require going in the open waters unless we took the cave passages. But do you know how dangerous those are? They're dark and cold and narrow. And there's no guarantee that that portal will work when we reach it. No one has entered the temple for decades."

"Mama said that the only reason that the portal hasn't worked on the grounded staircase is because the right runes aren't being used. I know how to make those. Or I can figure it out based on what she wrote." I flipped to the section where it listed reagents for the basin to empower the runes. They were relatively basic: stone, lavender, caraway, feathers, blood of the speaker, fire. Easy enough to obtain. Fire would be the hardest, but I had my flint. And I knew there was oilcloth in the storeroom. "And the portal would open up. We'd jump into the middle of the island and hold on to you long enough to open the portal up to another place. Then we'd jump through and sever the last of that bond!"

He shook his head, pushing the book down. "You don't comprehend how dangerous the cave paths are, darling. I can't guarantee that you'll come out alive on the other side."

"Does the cave path allow us to reach the temple without swimming through the open ocean or at least cut down on our time in the ocean?"

His jaw clenched. "You might not survive it. Risking the open waters, even with the leviathans and the water fae pursuing us, isn't as dangerous for you. And unlike in the caves, if something happens to me, you'd have a chance of reaching the surface while I dealt with them."

"You're fast, but I doubt you can swim faster than a leviathan." I gripped his hand.

His brow lifted slightly. Then he shrugged.

Son of a scallop! He hadn't planned on surviving at all. It wasn't just a high chance he wouldn't make it. My mate planned to lay down his life to save me.

I smacked his shoulder and glared at him. "Don't you dare come up with any more plans in which you die to save me. You said everyone always abandons you. Well, I'm not. So stop trying to abandon me. We finally found each other. I learn I'm your mate, and you expect me to just accept you're going to die? No!"

His eyes widened. His mouth trembled between a smile and a frown. "Mena—"

Tagger suddenly bolted back, screeching and squeaking. His hackles were raised as he stomped his feet.

Corvin's eyes went hard. He lunged at the door and raked his claws down the runic carvings along the panels. Light flared up, and something heavy ground into place. He'd barely gotten it done when the whole cavern shook.

We were out of time.

ESCAPE

I gripped Corvin's hand, my heart hammering against my ribcage harder than our attackers beat on the door. "The portal in the temple is our only chance. The only chance for both of us now."

His mouth twisted. A look akin to guilt flashed in his eyes and I wondered if he blamed himself for not getting me out of here sooner.

Another heavy thud struck the door as Lishen bellowed for Corvin to open the door.

"All right," Corvin said, his voice tight. He ran to the water entrance door, traced his claw over the runes a second time, and stepped back as the door glowed. The thuds weakened, as if the door had thickened.

"Corvin, open this door, or your suffering will increase a hundredfold!" Lishen snarled.

"A very painful death awaits me if any of you catch me," Corvin called back. "I have no reason to cooperate. Let the so-called hunt start here!" He then dragged one of the cupboards in front of the door.

As he did, I dug out some oilcloth and wrapped it around Mama's little book. What else would we need? I shoved the wrapped book into my pocket and gathered up the other reagents.

"Send word to the king of the traitor's acts," Lishen bellowed, loud enough for everyone to hear. "You will suffer, Corvin."

"I thought that was a given," Corvin jeered back. He braced his hands against a second cupboard as he shoved it forward, his expression far grimmer than his tone. "There will be no more harvesting my blood, marrow, or strength." He motioned for me to remain silent.

Did he really think he could fool them into believing I wasn't here?

Well, I wasn't going to fight him on that. I'd won on the most important point. We were going to escape together.

More curses followed as Lishen and his fae attacked.

As much as I hated it, I took some of the oily, salted fish along with two waterskins. I then took the daggers off Blue Ridges' corpse. Half of my wooden spoon remained embedded in his shoulder. My stomach twisted. Guess that was the end of my spoon.

I picked up the one part that remained on the floor and wrapped it as well before sticking it in the bag.

Tagger ran between Corvin and me as Corvin stacked and shoved cupboards and wood against the water way entrance. He stooped over Blue Ridges' body and signaled for me to get to the cave exit.

The heavy thuds continued, low and pounding as the snarls and curses intensified.

We'd also need something for a distraction. I ran to the stove and seized the heavy pot of stew. Corvin put something in his pocket as he studied me quizzically. "We can't eat stew on the run."

"No, but we can make it harder for them to tell where we're going," I said.

His eyes brightened, and he smiled. "You really are my clever girl."

As prepared as we could possibly be, we ran out into the darkness of the cave, pale-blue orbs in hand. Once through, Corvin traced his claw in the runic shapes along the iron band. Light flared, and the door seemed to tighten against the wall.

"I've poured every ounce of the magic reserved in the runes into holding these doors shut," he said in a hushed voice as he turned back to me. "If they aren't through in four hours, the runes will fail then. But they'll still have to get through everything else."

"Which passage are we taking?" I asked, holding the large pot of stew by the handles.

He gestured toward the narrowest one as he set aside the pale-blue orbs. Then he grabbed hold of the nearest boulder and dragged it to the door.

As he blocked the door, I ran into the openings of the other passages and spilled out the stew in generous quantities. I didn't put it in all of them. Only three. Enough that it looked as if we had started running, had a little accident, got confused, and ran back. To avoid leaving behind evidence, I tossed the stewpot into one of the pits. It clattered and banged its way down.

Oh, it hurt to be this wasteful.

Running back, I grabbed large rocks and chunks of marble as well, shoving them in the spaces around the boulders.

The thuds and curses had dulled, but they still vibrated through the cavern walls.

"How long do we have before those claws start going off

into your wrist?" I asked. Sweat already trickled down my brow.

"The king wanted me brought in alive. We've got maybe an hour before he realizes I've betrayed him. Unless he assumes Asha and her team betrayed him."

"His standard for betrayal is exceptionally low if he thinks this is betrayal," I muttered, wishing I could show this king what real betrayal looked like. I jammed another rock against the pile.

Corvin grunted as he dragged a jagged chunk of rock over. He braced it against the pile. "Yeah, well, for him, anything where we don't do precisely what he wants is betrayal."

"Are there other shifter fae like you near here?" Maybe we could find allies in this as well. I piled additional rocks on. Tagger brought his own contributions, squeaking and chirping.

Corvin shook his head. "Not close. Not after the accidents. This is one of the weaker boundaries anyway. As soon as I was old enough to hold the eel form for more than an hour, I was sent here. All the rest were sent to other boundaries for enforcement or similar tasks. The leviathans and other beasts under his control assisted in the patrols. We're on our own down here." He stepped back, his expression grim. He picked up the pale-blue orbs. "I'm getting you out of here, Mena. Whatever it takes."

"I accept that only if you go with me." The ferocity of my own feelings startled me. If anyone had told me last week that I'd feel this way for any man, I'd have laughed.

His gaze captured mine, and his expression softened. "Mena…"

Another heavy thud shuddered through the cavern.

His gaze flicked past me. Then he stiffened. He craned his head to look behind me.

I glanced back.

Oh.

An enormous crab drew closer, eyestalks bobbing, drawn by the shuddering vibrations. It didn't seem to notice us. Then it stopped at one of the puddles of stew and took a taste.

Corvin tugged at my arm and drew me down the narrowest side path.

No better sign for us to hurry. I hoped that crab stayed and ate Lishen and his fae.

"How far is the temple from here?" I asked as he guided me along. As much as I tried to keep my voice quiet, my own breaths sounded thunderous in my ears.

He ducked to avoid a column of stalactites. Some of the cave water dripped onto his shoulder. "Far enough. Watch your step."

He didn't hesitate as we plunged deeper and deeper into the caves. He was as much at ease in this space as he was in the ocean itself or as he had been on the ship.

I stumbled after him, trying to keep up as he led me through twisting passages and across narrow ledges. The pale light from the orbs cast eerie shadows that played tricks on my eyes. More than once, I nearly lost my footing on the uneven cave floor.

After what felt like an eternity of stumbling through the dark, we emerged into a massive cavern, so large I couldn't see the far side. Strange rock formations jutted up from the cave floor.

Had Lishen and his fae broken through yet?

Was it too much to hope that they would bring down a rockslide on themselves? Especially one that would trap only them.

"Is the mate bond going to make you immune to the venom in the claws?" I asked. Part of me had hoped we could get him through the portal in time, and then the magic that bound the claws to him would fall away and he wouldn't have to endure it.

"It'll probably be enough to keep it from killing me outright, but I'm still going to have to fight through and heal from it." Corvin massaged his wrist, his fingers pressing against the claws.

"And we can't, like, break the claws off?"

"If I try to break them off, they'll just stab me. I've tried many times," he said. He drew in a long, slow breath. "Taking in the venom all at once is much harder than bit by bit."

I shook my head.

The air had gone so still down here. It was stale and smelled more of minerals than anything. Places like this could go bad so fast. Sweat trickled down the neckline of my dress and the middle of my back. Nothing stirred.

He suddenly pointed to the left. "This way."

We only walked a few steps to the left when he stopped again in front of a puddle of dark water. He halted and adjusted his sleeves.

Wait.

What?

This?

"This is it?" I adjusted the bag over my shoulder, alarm flaring through me.

He gave me a sober look. "This is the start of passage that will get us to the temple. This cave system moves along most of the shallows in the North Sea."

"It's so small..."

He nodded as he crouched down. His claws grazed the still water, making it ripple. His gaze moved from the water to me. "Yeah. It's not the easiest path. Now you know why I didn't want you to have to take it with me." He sighed, his throat bobbing. "If something happens to me, you can use the runes to feel your way along."

I crouched beside him, searching for marks. If anything happened to him, I'd drag him through. We were getting through this together.

He took my hand and pressed it along the underside of the stone. My fingers slid against the grooves. They were deep, easy to feel at least.

"The runes guiding us to the temple have three lines and an arrowhead pointing in the opposite direction of the way we want to go." His expression remained solemn. "If the worst happens in there, they'll guide you out."

"Good to know. But you'll be with me." I said the last part with a hard emphasis, knowing he was implying that something was going to happen and I'd have to choose between living and saving him. "I'm not leaving you behind."

His brow remained furrowed. "We shouldn't delay." He glanced over at Tagger and snapped his fingers. "You follow close. Don't leave Mena."

Then it was my turn. His gaze held mine for a breath. I couldn't believe how intense the emotions that raged through me were. How much I wanted to be with him and near him. I put my arms around his neck and drew in a deep breath as I held the second of the pale-blue orbs.

Fear flared through me. My whole body tensed as I imagined sliding into the narrow, watery chasm.

"Try to relax if you can," he whispered, stroking my hair.

"How long will this part take?" My heart raced faster.

"It's…it's about two and a half miles. There are lots of air pockets. Remember the runes." With one more whispered word of encouragement, he then leaned forward and slid us into the dark water. It was so narrow he had to take us in headfirst.

That made it so much worse. The cold soaked around my

head while my legs twitched on the stone before Corvin dragged me into the narrow passage. All the warmth leeched from my bones within seconds. The stone scraped against my back. But it also pressed against the back of my hand which was against his neck.

Oh, Creator, help!

This—this was some sort of hell.

Corvin pressed us deeper into the dark waters, moving us through this tiny passage. Though his movements were smooth, I still felt the stones move beneath us and around us.

A thousand fears pecked at my mind.

It wasn't swimming. It was crawling underwater.

What if there was something else in these waters? What if we reached a blockage? What if the air pockets weren't there?

The tunnel constricted around us. Rocks scratched over my arms and back. Then a ledge pressed against the back of my head as Corvin wriggled us through.

I hated this. I hated it!

And I couldn't breathe.

I had to hold in screams and whimpers and panic. My lungs were already burning.

His arms tightened around me, his cheek pressed to mine.

We tilted up.

Our heads broke from the surface of the water.

I gasped and gulped in the air, my heart racing. A rock scraped the back of my head.

"Easy there," Corvin said, pulling me along.

The water shallowed here, the light coming solely from the orbs we carried. We were in a stone tube.

My feet and knees pressed against the coarse black stone. Ridges of rock pressed against the top of my head.

Tagger popped up beside us, chirping and squeaking. He

booped his nose against mine and then thrust his snout under my chin.

"This is...a very special kind of awful," I said, my teeth chattering. "Are they going to follow us in here? Can they?"

"It'll be tougher for them to track us. But yes. Ah!" Corvin gasped. His head slammed back against the wall with a sharp crack as his body spasmed. The orb dropped into the water.

DARK AND NARROW WATER
PATHS

I lunged for his orb, but it slid from my fingers, dropping from sight. Corvin lurched again, striking his head. I hit my head on the jagged ledge. Blood trickled from the scrape, but I barely felt it. The second orb faded from sight. "Corvin!"

He clutched his right hand to his chest.

Tagger nuzzled up against him, squeaking fearfully.

"What do you need?" Not that there was much I could do. "Do you want food? Will that help you heal faster?"

He drew in a sharp breath. "We'll have to hurry."

"How long before the next one strikes you?" I stared at him helplessly. "I couldn't save your orb!"

He shook his head. "I can time it out. Come on."

His arm shook as he wrapped it around my waist. I held on to him, drawing in a deep breath. His heart beat fast within his chest, so strong I could feel it with ease.

Down into the dark waters we went again.

The passage tightened. He wriggled along. I tried to mirror his movements, following his lead as I struggled not to panic. The water filled my nose and mouth.

Then we emerged.

We'd barely crept along the ledge before he fell back, gasping. His head banged the back of the wall, and his stripes went pale yellow and sickly green. The sharp scent of venom and blood reached my nostrils.

"I just—just have to fight through." He struggled to force a smile. "It's fine."

"Our mating bond—it's going to kick in soon and help you get full immunity, right?" I shivered in the water and glanced back at the narrow tunnel we'd crawled through. The bag hung heavy against my side.

He swallowed hard. "It's a little too soon for it to be there all the way," he said thickly. "It's changed enough that I've got —I've got a chance." He stroked my cheek, his fingers trembling. "Come on, clever girl. Don't give up on me now."

Tagger chittered his own commentary.

"I'm never giving up on you. Just breathe."

"I was thinking about stopping," he said, giving me a crooked grin.

Scowling, I smacked his shoulder. "Don't joke about that."

Tagger underscored my statement with a sharp trill. Neither of us wanted to think of anything happening to Corvin.

"Is there anything we can do to make the mating bond finalize faster?" I asked.

He shook his head. "It's going as fast as it can. That suppressant has to leave my blood. I could try bloodletting I suppose, but that's dangerous for other reasons. You being near me, though…that does help."

"How will we know when it's done?" I asked.

"Well, the mate bond may give you greater lung capacity and healing, among other things. It will strengthen us both." He nudged my cheek with his chin and kissed my forehead. "And for me, well, if everything changes then, I won't have these stripes or claws, and I'll be able to turn into something else."

"Something else?" My hand tightened around his. I tried to sound light and happy, hoping to encourage him. Right now, a peculiar combination of elation and terror cut through me. "What would you turn into?"

"Something with wings," he said. "I've always wanted to fly."

"Like a raven?"

"I was going to say dragon," he said with a weak laugh.

"Maybe a raven dragon," I suggested playfully, recalling the meaning of his name.

"Probably as likely as any other kind of dragon. My forms will likely be the forms that were strongest with my parents, and I don't know what those were. I don't know anything about them except what the king said, and…well, all of that is subject to doubt now." He leaned his head back against the cave wall, his breaths still rapid. His pulse throbbed visibly in his throat.

He took another few minutes to catch his breath. I stayed beside him, my whole body chilled from fear and the water. Then it was time. He guided me to another hole in the dark, and down we plunged again.

It was just as horrible as before. Maybe worse.

I couldn't keep track of time. But I knew it passed achingly slow. It was a nightmarish progression of crawling and swimming through water-filled tubes. More than once we almost got stuck. His heartbeat thundered against my ear, and his muscles trembled against me.

We slithered and crawled and crept through the tunnels. We'd barely reached the sixth air pocket before another claw deployed into Corvin's wrist. He groaned, driving his back against the wall and gritting his teeth.

I drew alongside him as close as I could, stroking his

shoulder as I watched him grip his wrist and struggle to heal around the bloodied puncture. The broken claws that had embedded into his flesh remained there, unforgiving reminders of his captivity. The remaining ones that curled against his wrist warned of future agony. Already he was so much paler.

"Come on." He winced as he tightened his arm around me. His panting intensified as he pushed me toward one of the narrow holes. "Have to—have to keep moving."

He didn't allow any arguments, and I knew there wasn't time. We wouldn't know if Lishen and his fae had managed to overtake us until it was almost too late. But feeling the rapid tattoo of his heart and the spasms in his muscles terrified me.

I tried to help our pace, wriggling in sync with him whenever we reached a tight point.

On and on we went, devastatingly slow.

The third claw deployed, sending him into rictal shudders. Exhaustion crept through me. Then, all too soon, the fourth claw bit. We barely made it up to an air pocket for that one as he gasped and choked, his body twitching. There were still three more to go.

Each time we surfaced, Tagger swept up against Corvin, whimpering and squeaking. I understood the feeling.

"I'm fine," he murmured through grey lips. But he forced down a mouthful of the fish and some of the fresh water, gagging.

Except he wasn't.

It had never occurred to me that someone like me could have a mate. I'd accepted my life was ordinary before Erryn went missing, and then I'd found myself thrust into an endless search that was shockingly mind-numbing despite all the close encounters with death.

My life changed within a matter of hours when Erryn vanished.

My life had turned over once again with Corvin. I wasn't going to lose him.

But right now…what could I do except support him and encourage him?

I hugged him tight as we navigated another set of tunnels. The cold numbed my hands and made my body heavy.

If the King of the North Sea wanted Corvin to suffer, he couldn't have asked for more. On and on we moved through dark waters. Three times we reached more open waters in the cave. Corvin moved slower and slower each time, but he guided us into the right passage each time.

This last time I felt his heartbeat racing faster, as if he had been running. Even with all my attempts to help, it wasn't enough. He was fading.

Somehow the lack of the stones around us and the wriggling through the chasm had become terrifying as well. I forced my eyes open as I felt his kicks weaken.

Then I saw it.

My blood chilled.

Below us moved pale lights. Lights like our orb. They were writhing in the space below us, wriggling through the tunnels.

I patted Corvin's shoulder and gestured downward, my lungs burning as if I had inhaled fire.

He twisted his head down as Tagger darted up. His muscles tensed, his arms tightening around me.

He pushed the orb into my hand. I took it in my numb fingers.

He kicked harder and faster, pushing us into a small passage that grated over my backside and thighs. I wriggled and pulled along with him, trying to help propel us into the next air pocket.

He spasmed, his head and back cracking against the coarse rock.

The other claw!

I tasted his blood in the water. Felt him go limp. His right side stopped moving completely, the arm about my waist loosening.

I seized him tight, the fingers of one hand digging into his tunic and the others wrapped tight around the pale-blue orb.

We weren't going to die down here.

Not like this!

I kicked and struggled, wriggling and tugging up—up —up.

My head broke the surface first. I jammed the pale-blue orb into a crevice in the wall above the water and dragged Corvin up the rest of the way.

He'd gone almost entirely grey. Water ran down his face, his lips parted. His hair covered his eyes. I had to drag him along the narrow tube to make room for Tagger to get up.

Tagger emerged, chattering and squeaking. He immediately nuzzled Corvin and nipped at his chin.

"Corvin, come on, it's all right," I rasped. I leaned him against the wall. The water was shallow enough we could sit. But something was coming. I could feel it.

Hands shaking, I groped in the water for a rock. Nothing moved. More holes opened up in the floor. Visions of something lunging up and snatching me filled my mind—sharp teeth, bulging eyes, heavy claws.

My shaking fingers at last found a rock that moved. I dragged it over to block the hole we'd crawled through. It slid partially through and then wedged into place. Bad news for anyone else. A flare of fear pulsed through me as I imagined encountering a similar obstacle.

Corvin's breathing had grown dangerously shallow. He trembled as if he had chills. "Mena," he whispered.

I curled against him, hugging him close. "You can do this. You can do this, Corvin. Just breathe through it. Breathe. Keep breathing! The mate bond is working. I could feel it when we were in the tunnel. My lungs aren't burning as much. That's got to mean you're getting closer too." Closer— and yet he still had more venom-dipped claws to go.

His left arm wrapped around me. He nuzzled me. "Runes —three slashes and the arrowhead," he murmured thickly. "Fifth chasm down. Two up."

I nodded, though my heart screamed. I wanted to be out of this place. Out of this tight, awful, cold darkness. My breaths shuddered in my chest as I put down those fears and stroked the hair back from his face. "I'm not leaving you."

"You should." He shook his head weakly. "Can barely feel the right side of my body. I'm sorry. It's time now, clever girl. Take Tagger. Get to—"

I kissed him. The salt of the water mixed with the salt of my tears as I held him tight. "I'm never leaving you."

He smiled weakly. "Tagger," he said, trying to pet the otter. "Tagger, if anything goes wrong, take Mena to air." His gaze slid to me, then his eyelids started to slide shut.

The *thud thud* of his heart had slowed. It wasn't as steady as it should be. I kissed him again and wished that there were some way for me to heal him. The best I could do was make sure we made it to the temple and we got through that portal. Then he'd be away from the King of the North Sea's magic.

Corvin's eyelids fluttered as he struggled to stay conscious. I turned his head so he wouldn't swallow more water, keeping him propped against me.

Tagger huddled against us, ears flat, gazing up at Corvin with sorrowful eyes. He gave a soft, squeaking whine, and I swore he was asking what he could do to help. I wished I had an answer.

A small vibration pulsed through the water.

The something was closer.

I swallowed hard. "Come on, Corvin. Deep breaths for me, please. We've got to go."

He nodded weakly.

I started fumbling about in the dark water, searching for the holes to count. One. Two. Three.

Another vibration pulsed up. Stronger this time.

"Mena," Corvin said, his voice cracking. He struggled forward. "You missed—" He slipped and plunged into darkness.

WRONG CHASM

"Corvin!" I screamed.

Tagger had already shot down the chasm after him, slicing into the dark water like a blade.

I seized the pale-blue orb, took in a deep breath, and plunged in headfirst.

This chasm was wider and more open, its mouth easily large enough for me to slip through.

My eyes stung and blurred from the salt water, but there was no doubt. Either my vision had improved from the mate bond, or desperation had given me strength. I prayed it was the mate bond because that meant maybe I could hold my breath longer.

The light pierced through the dark chasm.

There!

Corvin drifted limply ahead of me, dark hair fanning out. Blood trickled from a gash on his head and his wrist. His left leg twitched. Tagger circled him, pawing at his head and nudging up under his chin.

Panic surged through me. I swam faster, kicking down. The bag around my shoulder tugged against me, sometimes snagging on the ridges. I wriggled and twisted until I reached Corvin. Sweeping my arm around him as best I could, I dragged us up.

I was moving fast, but where were we supposed to go? Was I even going the right way?

Everything looked the same down here. The pale-blue light illuminated the chasm with its gnarled rock formations, but I couldn't tell what was a passage. And I had to find the second one. Except—no, we weren't in the right chasm at all, were we?

I struggled, kicking and fighting. My whole body screamed for air and space. I just held on to him and swam as Tagger zipped around us.

Then we broke the surface. A sharp pain struck the top of my head.

There was barely enough room for our heads above the water.

It was enough though, the air not the best but still breathable.

Spitting out the water, I hacked and gasped as I pulled Corvin up. The rough rocks pressed against my skull. The salt water stung all my cuts and scrapes.

Corvin choked too, but his breaths were still weaker. He almost slipped back under.

Tagger chittered anxiously beside me. We had to get Corvin out of here. But which way?

The runes.

I started fumbling about below the waterline. My fingertips found one set of runes. Two slashes and a circle.

I groped along to the next wall, searching wildly. Another set of runes, all wrong. How many were down here?

Tagger swam in tight circles around us, squeaking. He darted under my hand and then shot into the dark water.

I pulled Corvin with me along the gap that allowed us to

breathe, struggling to support him and hold up the orb and feel for runes. My fingers ached. The weight of the water against my lungs hurt.

Tagger popped up again. He squeaked louder, then seized the orb from my hand.

"Tagger, no!" I tried to grab for him, but he had already dived under, taking our only light source with him.

This was it. The air here wouldn't last long anyway.

I didn't have any other choice.

I wrapped my arms around Corvin, urged him to take a breath, and then pulled us both under.

Tagger swam a few feet below. Even through my blurred vision, I could make him out with the orb. He didn't swim as swiftly now. But he kept a steady pace, just out of my reach. He darted up to a different passage.

I followed. Corvin wasn't even struggling. His left arm kept enough of a grasp on me that I knew he was alive. But his muscles trembled. His wrist bled into the water.

Tagger arched gracefully into the hole in the rock, treading water with the orb between his paws. His withered paw had to hug it a little tighter while the ordinary paw overlapped it.

He led us up to another air pocket, this one with a little more headspace but without any rocks beneath to serve as a rest point. Still, I appreciated the air. Corvin managed a few more shuddering breaths.

Tagger squeaked, bobbing his head up and down and splashing as he held the pale-blue orb.

"We have to get to the temple," I said wearily. I didn't know how much longer I could swim.

Tagger dove down.

Damn it!

Did he understand what I was saying? I gulped in another breath, warned Corvin, and then dove again.

It became a terrifyingly slow waltz swimming as Tagger led me into different passages. The fifth claw jammed into Corvin's wrist just as we reached the surface of another tunnel. He managed a weak groan.

"If you die on me, I'm never going to forgive you," I growled.

He murmured something nonsensical in response.

I groped around in the dark, feeling for the runes. None of them matched. How many passages were in this place?

Despair threatened to overwhelm me. It felt as if we had been in this place forever. My mouth was dry, my lips chapping, my body aching.

Then I glimpsed it. Another light. Brighter blue. It was coming from one of the lower tunnels.

Panic surged through me. I kicked faster, following Tagger to a honeycomb of passages. As we struggled up, I searched for any runes on the craggy rock walls.

Wrong.

Wrong.

Wrong!

Tagger cut to the right where the passage branched.

The light faded, but there—there!

I'd seen it!

Three slashes and an arrowhead.

I struggled to draw Tagger's attention as I kicked toward the passage.

He swept around, squeaking and chirping. He rushed toward me in a cloud of bubbles as I gestured feebly at the passage ahead, my kicks getting weaker.

Tagger shot forward, clutching the orb close.

Higher. Higher.

A deep vibration pulsed beneath me.

I twisted around just enough to see shadowy movement at the edge of the light.

This was so bad. How much time did we have before they caught up?

We broke through the surface. Tagger chattered. He swam up to me.

A small hole looked as if it opened into another passage. The three slashes and an arrowhead were boldly carved above the mouth.

Still supporting Corvin, I swam toward that point and struggled up. "Tagger." My voice shook. "I need the orb." I held out my hand rather than trying to grab it from him.

With a few squeaks, he dropped it in my palm and then darted back in front of Corvin's face. He nuzzled his chin and started grooming him, making Corvin startle a little.

"Just hang on." I set my foot against a groove in the rock and pushed myself up high enough to illuminate the passage. It moved farther up, perhaps three feet or so. Then it opened. Cut deep into the side near the top was the rune with the three slashes and the arrowhead.

The temple. It had to be on the other side. "We're here!" I gasped.

Corvin mumbled. His stripes had gone entirely grey, his lips almost black. He wasn't going to be able to climb up easily.

We were so close.

"Just hang on," I said, gasping. My heart raged within my ribcage. I wedged him against the wall and started to climb.

It was a tight squeeze. I had to remove my bag and fit it into one of the indentations. The rough rock scraped my knees and elbows. My breaths filled my ears. And then I was through the slick rock, pale-blue orb held aloft.

My mouth fell open.

We weren't outside a temple. This passage opened up inside it. Cracked marble tiles covered the floor. The pearly white contrasted sharply with the black craggy tube I'd crawled out of. The temple itself had been carved from marble. Carved columns supported portions of the ceiling, though quite a few had cracked and fallen. Whole sections of the wall had shorn off, exposing the cave walls beneath, glistening with water. I recognized some of the markings on the pillars from Mama's book.

Wriggling out of the hole, I leaned back in and reached for the bag. My fingers narrowly hooked the strap. I tossed it up onto the marble.

"Corvin, we're here! We made it," I shouted. "Come on."

The passage was only wide enough for one of us at a time. Even then it was going to be an especially tight squeeze for him.

He struggled to open his eyes. "Mena, go on ahead. I'll—I'll catch up."

"No." I knew better than that. "Get out of the water. You've got to fight more. I can't carry you the whole way." He was too heavy for me to lift without some help. Especially at this level. The venom was shutting him down completely. The fact that he had survived this long was a miracle, but we needed another one fast.

He nodded, his breaths slow and uneven. Blood leaked from his wrist. Not a trace of yellow or green was left in his skin, and his lips and a fair portion of the surrounding skin had gone ink-black or spiderwebbed with dark veins now. His eyelids remained heavy. But he tried again, his muscles trembling and shaking as he forced himself forward.

Slowly he made his way up, leaning heavily against the wall as I reached down for him.

Bubbles churned within the water. A pinprick of light shone below.

Something was coming. And fast.

It wasn't hard to guess what.

"Tagger, up!" I snapped my fingers at him, using the sharpest tone I'd ever used.

This time, he didn't even squeak or protest. He shot up the tunnel and past me as if he had been greased.

I then crawled back down into the hole, reaching for Corvin. "Corvin, do *NOT* argue with me. If you've got any strength left, you've got to help me get you out of here. Otherwise, I'm coming back in, and we can both die together. Do you want that?" My fingertips grazed his shoulder. His right arm hung limp.

He struggled to turn and thrust himself up. He slipped.

I lunged farther down into the passage headfirst, hoping I didn't fall in. The rocks cut into my belly and thighs. I just barely caught his sleeve, grunting with pain.

He fought to stand again, his muscles clenching.

Salt's bane, it wasn't just his right arm. His leg was giving out too.

He swung his hand up into the passage, his claws digging into the grooves.

I tugged and pulled. His claws cut my arm, though he couldn't grip my arm back. His blood dripped down his wrist onto me, mixing with mine. The sharp pain sliced through me, but I couldn't let go. I wouldn't.

He struggled up a little higher, and I wriggled back, pulling him with me.

Inch by painful inch.

He was so heavy and weak that I could barely budge him.

"Just a little more!" I cried out, my muscles burning with effort.

Tagger chittered, darting around the opening. He settled on my back to help me balance. His loud chirps and squeaks filled my ears in counterpoint to Corvin's labored breaths. "Come on!"

His body blocked out all view into the chasm below. But whatever was coming up had to be close by now.

He groaned, his voice tearing into me as I clung to him. The muscles in his arms trembled.

"Almost there!" I wriggled back still farther and then gripped more of his arm. "You're more than halfway."

He grunted, all movement stopping. Alarm flashed in his eyes.

It only took me a moment to see the problem.

His shoulders were stuck, and something was coming up the tunnel.

THE PORTAL

"*M*ena—" Corvin started.

"So help me, if you suggest I leave you behind, I will bite you," I snapped. But inside I was panicking. We had to get him out. But that would mean lowering him down into the tunnel again and then having him drop his shoulder at an awkward angle so that I could drag him up the rest of the way. An idea snapped into my mind.

"Brace yourself. I'm going to let go of you for just a moment," I said.

He nodded weakly. Sweat and salt water poured down his face, plastering his hair to his head. The light in his emerald-green eyes had faded so much, and his fingertips had gone ink-black. But he was still fighting, even as the breaths shuddered from his body.

Dashing forward, I seized my bag and dumped the contents onto the marble floor. They spilled out, a few items rolling. Tagger chased after them, herding them back.

I grabbed the bag and brought it over to him, stretching out the strap. "You're going to lower yourself down and we're going to use this to help you get up again, all right? You're going to have to put both your arms up as straight as possible. But it's going to pinch your shoulders."

Something thudded below him. The vibration pulsed through the floor.

Panic surged through me.

"Clever," he murmured weakly.

"All right. Let's do it. One. Two. Three." I strained as I helped him ease back down.

His face twisted with pain. I helped him maneuver, my heart hammering.

He lowered down as the vibration pulsed louder. We got the strap of the bag around him and he forced his other arm up, though now his body twisted at an awkward angle while the limp arm hung down.

Hoarse laughter echoed up from below him.

I tugged harder.

His body twisted up another inch or so, his claws digging into the stone as I pulled with all my strength.

"Cut him!" one of the deep voices shouted.

"Can you get free, flesh scraps?" another laughed. That sounded like Black Claws.

"Test his strength," another called out among the gurgling and bubbles.

Corvin struggled harder. Sweat rolled down his cheeks. His eyes had lost most of their color. Even his teeth were starting to go grey.

How many of them could fit down there? I clenched my jaw and tugged.

He arched, the inkiness in his fingertips and lips spreading into veins along his mouth and up his arms. The scent of blood blossomed in the air, sickening me.

They were hurting him!

I knotted my hands around the straps and tugged harder.

More laughter followed. They jerked him down and then released him.

Corvin's muscles strained. He jammed his left arm against the marble, the veins in his brow and neck bulging.

I heaved with all my strength, adrenaline granting me more might than I had ever had. Corvin's body grated and twisted through the narrow opening, one shoulder snapping out of its socket.

Angry curses followed from below. Black Claws had gotten wedged in part of the way up. His eyes sparked with rage and hatred. "Filthy human whore!" he spat. "You can't escape us!"

Using his one good arm, Corvin dragged himself across the marble tiles. Several knife and claw wounds had gashed into his legs. His right hand pressed to his chest, the fingers now black all the way to the palm. With a grunt of pain, he snapped the shoulder back into place.

I grabbed one of the fallen rocks and chucked it into the pit. It struck Black Claws in the face. As he yelped, I found another and flung it in. Tagger pushed in gravel and smaller bits of rock. It only took a few minutes to jam up the entrance. And that pinch point was low enough in the mouth of the tunnel to make it difficult for them to just shove the debris out of the way. Especially when I packed it in.

The rageful shouts and bellows below grew more muffled.

This wasn't the only entrance point. I was certain of that. And now that they knew where we were, they'd likely be here soon.

I ran to him, dropping to his side. Blood spilled onto the marble as he struggled to heal. One of the largest wounds in his thigh had barely closed. I tried to rip my skirt to make bandages, but the damp fabric refused to tear.

"No, it's fine. Just a moment." He placed his hand over one of the wounds.

He wasn't healing fast enough. He was barely keeping himself alive.

I pulled out the dagger from his belt and used it to cut the fabric. "It'll help to put pressure on the wound. Then you can heal it. Besides, after we get out of this, I assume you'll want to see my legs, so who cares if my skirt gets shredded a little early?"

He tried to smile. "Your legs are magnificent."

"You haven't even seen them yet," I teased, trying to keep my tone light. I glanced at the pile of stones in the hole. "Do you know where there are other entrances? How fast can they get here?"

He gestured weakly toward the end of the passage beyond us. "There's another entrance there. They'll have to go back down."

I started to bind up the wounds on his leg. He didn't even twitch his right leg. The smell of blood and salt water filled my nostrils. "How long?"

"I—I don't know—" He moistened his lips. His tongue had gone grey too. Almost like charcoal.

"Do you need food? Water?" I grabbed the wrapped oiled fish and the waterskin, thrusting it against him. The packet fell to the floor as the waterskin sloshed.

"If there's any chance of you getting through the portal, you need to start on that," he said, panting. "Don't…don't worry about me."

Don't worry about him? He was half dead already! How could I not worry about him? But what good did worrying do when we had so little time?

We only had the one light source left. I grabbed the oilcloth-wrapped book and removed it. The pages flipped open toward the back. Rifling through the pages, I searched for what I knew would help. Mama had made a map.

There was a map in here. A very bare one. But a map!

I scanned the page, then looked back at him. "Then it should be down this hall if Mama got it right." The map didn't actually show the access point we had taken. What if there were others? No, I needed to just focus.

"Take the light." He continued to press his hand against the wounds on his legs, his breathing ragged.

"I'm coming back for you." I kissed his forehead. His skin held only the barest traces of warmth, but he gripped my arm in response, nodded, then gave me a gentle shove.

"Go."

I staggered forward, steeled myself, then ran. I would come back.

The pale-blue orb nestled cold in my palm. I grabbed the journal and padded down the hall, scanning the doorways. Whole sections of marble had fallen away, some in pieces at the base and others smashed across the floor.

My footsteps and breaths echoed in the cold of this place. It seemed to stretch on and on without end.

There! The runes in the arched doorway matched the ones in the book.

I stepped inside, heart pounding. The doors had been shoved open and now sagged against the wall. Some great fight had happened here long ago. Dark streaks like dried blood stained the stone. Four corpses lay on the ground, their clothing tattered and rotted. Burnt-out torches lay by two. Chunks of rock and a shattered column littered the floor.

The staircase with its intricate carvings dominated the back of the room. Urns and braziers, long since empty, stood at intervals, with an especially large one at the top of the staircase before a broad platform.

The air now held a bite to it. Something like death and dust and lightning mixed together as one.

But it was here.

We had a chance. I shoved the book back into my pocket and ran.

Corvin was already struggling in my direction. He hugged the wall, dragging himself along. His right leg barely supported him, and he had to be moving simply on will. Blood dripped from the wounds. With hardly any light left in his eyes and his hair flat against his skull, he was unrecognizable.

Tagger squeaked and circled him. But even the otter's voice was softer now, as if he too was nearing despair.

Running to Corvin, I slid under his right arm and helped lift him up. His weight almost dropped me.

Just a little farther. The light from the orb cast flickering shadows on the wall, slashed by my fingers as I gripped it and struggled forward.

So close.

His ragged breaths barely warmed my skin as his head sagged against mine. His body was like ice, his pulse thready. Black veins raced up his neck and over his temples.

"You—you don't look good."

He shook his head. His attempt at a smile failed, his panting making it all the worse. "Looks worse than it is."

I scoffed. How much worse could it get before he died? "Yeah, well…" I gestured toward the archway, indicating where we were going to go. "You really—you look bad." My gaze dropped once more to his right hand. His whole hand had gone black, and dark liquid dripped from his claws. Could he even survive the last claw punching into his wrist?

"Just—think of it like going to sleep and restoring. If I get through, I'll be—I'll be reborn," he said, his voice shaking.

"What happens if it's too much for you?" I staggered a little as another muscle tremor nearly took him down.

"Well...I guess I don't wake up." His voice broke as his gaze dropped to my bloodied arms where my sleeve was riding up. "Was this me? Did I do this?"

"No. It's fine. I'm fine." I tugged him forward, struggling under his weight. "You'll be fine."

There was still one more venom-dripped claw. The mate bond between us had supported and strengthened me, but it wasn't enough for him yet. How could he survive yet another dose with all this blood loss?

We had to get him through the portal.

This temple was so much smaller and less impressive than what I'd expected. But I was glad that we didn't have far to stagger before we reached the chamber with the staircase and the portal.

Setting Corvin down, I placed the orb beside him. Tagger sniffed Corvin and curled up against him, squeaking more.

The doors.

I had to get the doors shut.

The king's warriors would be here soon. And when they arrived, well—we really weren't in any condition to fight. I'd fought off bandits before, but not in situations like this. The sagging doors resisted at first, but I pushed each one shut, then twisted the warped lock as far into place as I could.

Corvin gestured toward the staircase. "I'll shore up the doors." He motioned toward some of the urns and furniture as well as the cracked columns and stones that had fallen near the doors.

I ran to the top of the staircase, my footsteps echoing around me as Corvin grunted and huffed. He struggled to push the broken stone against the doors. Pebbles and rubble crunched beneath his feet. It looked like he might pass out against it.

But I had to focus on this stage. If we didn't get the portal working, we were dead anyway. There was nowhere else for us to go.

A fine layer of dust filled the wide-mouthed basin at the top of the staircase. My nerves tingling, I set the bag down and the orb down and squinted at the page. It took only a few minutes to grab the materials and combine them. The wood had only gotten a little wet on one end. And the blood —well, I was already bleeding from his claws in my arm.

I made the fire and dropped the flames into the basin, then dipped my fingers in my own blood and mixed it with the ash to mark out the runes on the archway and sides of the staircase on the platform as the book instructed.

The runes in the staircase lit up with pale-blue light, similar to the orb. The entire room was bathed in its peaceful glow. That lightning-like scent intensified, sharp and bright. The light built and grew at the end of the platform before the staircase, and the air crackled before a mirror-like opening appeared.

My heart leaped.

Yes!

It was working!

The portal looked out into a sandy-soiled forest during what looked like the afternoon. A camp had been set up around the staircase. And there—a familiar form huddled on the stairs, her moss-green shawl wrapped tight around her shoulders. A small broken mug and a bit of fish sat on a leaf on the lower step. As the portal hissed into existence, Mama sat up, her eyes widening. She jumped up and raced to the platform, her voice sounding like it came from the end of a tunnel. "Philomena!"

"Mama!" My breath caught in my throat, and tears filled my eyes. I smiled even though I was scared because I was so happy to see her. All I wanted to do was hug her. "Mama, it worked! The portal worked!"

"It did!" Her eyes widened, and her hand clapped over her mouth. "It's working. It worked! All you have to do is walk through." She gestured for me to come through. "Hurry, darling. Hurry!"

"Corvin, get up here. Tagger!" I gestured for them wildly. Tagger bolted up the stairs, squeaking and chirring. He halted at my feet, rising up on his hindquarters as he sniffed the air.

Mama's face fell, her hand covering her mouth. "It's not just you?"

My heart sank. The soft way she said that. Dread nipped at my mind. "No. Corvin is with me. He's the reason I'm here. And Tagger." I brushed my fingers over the otter's head.

Mama pressed her hand to her mouth, seeming to almost shrink inward as her brow creased. "Oh, sweetheart, this portal—it's only strong enough to transport one."

UNDERSTOOD

*T*hose words might as well have been daggers. They stabbed right through me.

"What?" I stared at her.

"The strength of the magic between these two portals is limited," Mama said, her gaze fixed on me. "This one can only take one person. Maybe you could carry the otter through. But it isn't strong enough for two people to be transported safely."

Corvin sat at the bottom of the staircase, shaking his head. He opened his mouth to speak when a heavy thud battered the doors.

They were here.

No!

My gaze locked with Corvin's, sadness and resignation filling his now-dull eyes. But the slightest of smiles tugged at his mouth. "I'll hold them off, clever girl. They're coming for me anyway. Let them have my blood and let me know you have survived. Just take Tagger and go."

Tagger squeaked with alarm. He raced down the stairs to

Corvin. Putting his paws on Corvin's chest, he chuffed and nipped at him.

I agreed wholeheartedly. "No! I have given up so much that I have wanted, and I won't give up you."

Mama's voice came from the portal, shaky not just from magic but emotion. "Sweetheart, he can open another portal and get through that."

Except he couldn't. He was barely holding himself up on the stairs. His breaths came in ragged pants, his left hand wrapped around his right wrist as if he could somehow hold off that last injection of poison. Should I send him through this one and figure out another way? No. Even if he got onto the island, it would still be close enough to the King of the North Sea that his power would remain, and the island staircase portal wouldn't be strong enough to allow us to escape elsewhere for who knew how long?

We needed a portal staircase somewhere farther away. Somewhere we could both go.

The doors shook again. The attackers on the other side cursed and swore, their voices muffled but irate. The stones grated on the floor, the heavy rubble holding it shut. But it wouldn't last. They'd be through in minutes.

"Philomena!" Mama's voice cut through the air. "Be reasonable, sweetheart. You cannot delay any further. Get yourself through this portal right now. I've already lost Erryn. I won't lose you too. Let him have the pages in the book and he can find his own way through another."

"No." I swallowed hard as I turned back to Mama. "No, I will not leave him. Can you tell me another portal staircase we can reach from here?"

Mama's lips pressed into a tight line. She gave me that look. That look that told me she expected me to listen.

I didn't care.

I'd backed down on so much to make her happy. I'd given

up everything to find Erryn and to take care of Mama. But no more. Maybe dreams were only going to lead to disappointment, but I was finally going to ask for what I wanted for me.

"Mena," Corvin whispered, laying down on the stone. "Just go."

No.

No!

"If you hurry up and come through, he'll have the time to make it to another portal," Mama said in her most soothing and persuasive voice. "Please. Please hurry, sweetheart."

My face hot, I turned to face Mama. "Mama, I love you, but I won't leave him. I have given up everything else I cared about. I haven't even tried to have a life. I don't even know how much of a life I'm going to have left, but I won't give him up."

Everything faded as we stared into each other's eyes. I wanted to say so much. So many words. And all that came out next was a strangled "please."

It wasn't much. Just a single, shaking syllable.

Tears brimmed in her eyes as she looked right at me. Then she nodded at the book in my hand. "You have my book? Turn to page eighty-one."

Hands trembling, I flipped through. The descriptions and coordinates on this page detailed those of another grounded portal and staircase.

"Draw those symbols on the arch and in the basin as you did for this one. That one should be strong enough." Mama placed her hand at the base of her throat, her voice shaking. "It's at Gryphon's Crossing. We can reach you there, or you can start on the west road and we'll find a place between."

I nodded, choking. "Thank you. I love you, Mama. Your research—it's impressive." There was so much more I wanted to say.

The doors shuddered.

"That portal is one of the strongest ones," Mama said. She covered her mouth. "I love you, sweetheart. I love you, and I'm proud of you." Her hand shaking, she then pressed it over the portal's center, and it faded.

Part of me couldn't believe she'd agreed. That she had given me the answer. And part of me knew why she had.

More heavy thumps and cracks struck the door. We didn't have much time, but I didn't need long.

Corvin continued to struggle up the staircase. He was over halfway there.

"I'm not leaving you behind, I promise," I called down to him. "I'm just going to prepare this."

I picked up the reagents from my bag and added them to the basin. Seeds, feathers, and flowers spilled in.

I had enough of everything except—wood.

Where had the other piece gone? Had it fallen out when I dumped the bag?

I scanned the chamber floor, searching desperately for the missing piece of wood. The pounding on the door grew louder, the lock beginning to buckle.

Corvin dragged himself up another step, but he was fading fast. "What's wrong?" he rasped.

"Come on, come on," I muttered, digging through my bag again just in case I had missed it. Still nothing.

My fingertips brushed my broken spoon wrapped in the oil cloth.

My heart twinged as I grabbed it.

It was splintered and jagged, but it was also flammable and dry. Shaking my head, I jammed it into the dying sparks of the previous fire. It smoldered, the smoke curling higher.

The doors shuddered once more. A gap of pale light appeared in a line as the columns rocked. One of the warriors tried to jam his hand through the crack.

I mixed the reagents into the basin. The flames caught. The spoon burned, the wood crackling and popping. I poured in the seeds, the lavender, and everything else. The scents merged in a heady blend. The cuts on my arm had almost stopped bleeding, but I scratched at them to let the blood trickle into the basin.

"Just hang on, Corvin," I said, my voice shaking. I referred back to the book as I traced the symbols onto the beams and the arch. The portal started to light up.

The doors thudded again. The pounding echoed through the chamber.

With a strangled cry, Corvin spasmed on the staircase. The final claw had embedded in his wrist.

"Corvin!" I screamed.

Tagger screeched with me. His high-pitched squeaks filled the air. He circled and pounced on Corvin, his little paws striking his chest and face.

Corvin didn't move.

DESPERATION

I raced down the last four stairs to Corvin and crouched beside him, not even watching as the portal came to life once more. "Corvin? Corvin!"

I jammed my fingers against his throat. No pulse greeted me. Not even a thready one. His skin was like ice.

Tagger squeaked and cried, thrusting his face against Corvin's.

All I wanted to do was lay down and sob. To curl up on his body and mourn for what might have been. My body ached. Everything was cold. The darkness intensified, suffocating and powerful.

The doors shook and grated, the steady slamming on the door and foul curses sworn with each blow.

The portal continued to form.

Sunlight poured through the portal, mixing with the pale-blue of the runes and the orb. A golden afternoon in a birch forest in the mountains. Birdsong reached me through the hum of the portal over the grunting and shouting of the warriors fighting their way through the door.

Then it flickered.

Wait.

Was this one not stable either? What if Mama was wrong?

I set my jaw.

It didn't matter. This was our one way out. As long as Corvin, Tagger, and I went through together, we'd go to the same place.

There was no way in the abyss or the expanse that I'd leave Corvin behind. Not even if he really was dead.

I stooped down, grabbed his arm, and dragged him up. "Come on. Tagger. We're getting out of this place."

Tagger squeaked faster, his high-pitched voice frantic as he raced around me. He hopped on Corvin and nudged him, then ran up the stairs and looked at me.

Corvin's body sagged against the stairs. I dragged him up, focusing on each step, grunting as we moved toward the portal.

With a deafening *crack*, the doors finally splintered open. Lishen and his three warriors forced their way in.

Lishen's eyes glowed as he pointed at me. "Halt, whore!" Black Claws and two others shoved in behind him. They had their swords and daggers drawn. As if they couldn't tear me apart with their claws and teeth.

"Tagger, come on," I gasped.

Almost there!

Tagger hopped up on to Corvin's chest, squeaking.

Something sharp clipped my shoulder and stung like a hornet. I startled.

What? How?

A dart stuck in my shoulder.

Oh. Oh, salt's bane!

The edges of my vision fuzzed. Heat burned through my arm.

I staggered forward, wincing under Corvin's weight as I glanced back.

More warriors poured into the room. One stood on the far side of the room, readying another dart. The other had reached the base of the stairs. Lishen and Black Claws were halfway up the stairs, thundering toward me, eyes blazing.

No!

I lunged forward as best I could, pulling Corvin with me. The portal crackled and flared around us.

My foot caught on the ledge. Tagger and Corvin fell out along with me. We struck the stone platform and rolled. The dart twisted in my arm.

The ground fell away. Plants and branches along the side of the platform and stairs struck my face as we rolled down.

Hackles bristling, Tagger leaped.

We crashed, rolled, and slid down the staircase. Corvin slid away from me. My hand grabbed for his arm. My fingers raked over his throat.

Did I feel a pulse?

His body slipped to the side.

No, please, wait!

I couldn't hold on to him.

Couldn't even scream as I skidded down the stone. Blood filled my mouth. The edges of the stairs scraped and gashed my legs and arms. The world tumbled around me. Somehow I clutched something. My bloodied fingers raked over the surface.

Something seized me by the back of the head, digging into my scalp. It hauled me up, bending me back.

I screamed in pain.

Black Claws stood over me. He'd come through the portal. But where were the rest? Was he alone? Had it closed in time?

I clawed at him and struggled to break free. "Your reward, you human whore," he snarled, lifting his hand. A blade flashed. "Did you really think you could escape?"

My breath caught. I lifted my arm to grab his wrist. He moved to slash at my throat.

A blur of dark fur sprang onto his face, knocking him back as the blade nicked the side of my neck. Tagger bit down on the bridge of his nose, his eyes blazing.

Black Claws screamed. My hand remained wrapped around his wrist, and I wrenched the dagger back away from him, then fell back, unable to close my fingers around the handle. The edges of my vision got fuzzier.

Black Claws released it and grabbed at the furious otter, but Tagger had latched on, his claws digging into the sides of the fae's face as he gnawed and shrieked.

Black Claws staggered back, teetering on the edge.

I shoved myself up, put out my arm, and struck my shoulder to show the otter where to go. "Tagger!"

Tagger leaped like a cat and landed squarely on my shoulder as I struck Black Claws and shoved him off the edge of the staircase. Black Claws crashed over the edge with a rage-filled shriek.

Staggering back, I started to turn, my chest heaving.

An arm slammed me into the wall.

Tagger fell off as well with an angry squeak.

I barely drew in a breath before my attacker struck me. The rough metal of his bracers cut into my chest and against my throat.

Lishen!

Pure hatred burned in his eyes. A sneer twisted his face. Then he struck me in the chest, the blade cutting deep before he ripped it back. Behind him came the other warriors, pouring out of the portal.

All the wind was driven from my lungs. I couldn't even scream. All I managed was a wheezing gasp.

"What did you do to her?" a deep, familiar voice raged from above.

Corvin? It sounded like him and yet not. As if he had changed and gotten higher than us. I tried to twist my head around to see him. Pain sliced through me, then dulled as I faded. My blood pounded in my ears. Lishen shoved me against the wall again, his fist wrapped in my bloodied dress.

Heat blossomed in my chest.

I was far away now.

So far away.

Blood filled my mouth, but even its taste faded.

Shadows pulled at my vision, and Lishen filled my sight.

Lishen snarled at him. "She's already dead, flesh scraps. What—"

A massive reptilian roar followed along with the infuriated, lecturing squeaks of an otter.

A dragon? That was a dragon. A dragon with an otter?

Lishen's eyes widened, his nostrils flaring as every muscle in his body tensed.

He dropped me to the staircase and reached down for his sword.

But it was too late.

A black-feathered dragon lunged onto him, thunderous in response as he reached for his sword. Feathers and scales and a hooked black beak and glittering green eyes.

I stared.

That—he—Corvin *was* a raven dragon.

I watched through hazy vision as he attacked, his claws raking over Lishen's chest and sending him sailing. The other two fae attacked, their blades slicing at his feathers. The feathers fell away, catching the sunlight with iridescent radiance.

He dispatched them with equal ease. One by one, each one fell. Some torn apart, others flung.

I slumped down against the stone. The world was fading too fast.

And I was tired.

So tired.

He didn't know about the poisoned dart.

I couldn't even speak. Could barely breathe.

And...I hated this.

But not as much as I might have.

This was where it would end.

Once more, I had no voice.

But the sun was on my face, warm and golden.

I could—I could see him.

He was flying. And he was glorious.

And we weren't going to die in that wretched cave.

What was it he had said about falling asleep? That's what this felt like.

He spread his wings as he tossed another of our attackers off the cliff. The hints of green and yellow in the feathers were only afterthoughts of color, similar to the iridescent traces of color on a grackle or a starling.

Then he spun in the air, and his gaze fell on me once more. His bright-green eyes widened.

He saw me. "Mena!"

Darkness misted my vision, leaving only those bright-green eyes burning.

Tired. Heavy.

My eyelids slid shut.

SEEN

ir flooded my lungs, and energy surged into my fingertips.

Gentle fingers without claws pressed against my cheeks and neck.

It was as if my eyelids had millstones on them. The scent of salt, blood, fresh air, and green leaves filled my nostrils. That, and something muskier and heavier. Familiar, even if the touch wasn't.

"Come on. Wake up, clever girl. Open those gorgeous eyes. You took on all those men. I don't think you thought that through, but I know you're here. You wouldn't leave me. Not now."

Corvin?

His voice was gentle and teasing all at once. His lips brushed my forehead, then pressed against my cheek.

Slowly I opened my eyes and met his gaze. I froze. The man peering down at me... "Corvin?" I whispered.

His skin was no longer striped with yellow and green. He was deeply tanned now, his cheekbones and jaw even more exquisitely sculpted, and his eyebrows strong and proud. No claws protruded from his fingers. He was even more breath-takingly handsome, and all that intensity and need in his brilliant gaze was focused on me.

He held me in his arms. We sat in a clearing near the stone staircase and the portal. But the portal at the top of the staircase had closed, the runes no longer glowing and the basin upturned.

He touched my cheek with his fingertips. "Yes, it's me." The smile that lit up his face had such joy. It crinkled around his eyes. "Hello, clever girl."

"I'm not dead."

Tagger squeaked and popped up, prodding me with his cold nose. I giggled as his whiskers tickled me.

"No, you're stuck with me," he whispered.

Tagger trilled again.

"Fine." Corvin chuckled. "With both of us." He stroked my cheek, his fingers curling against my skin. "Darling, I have to tell you...I'm rather obsessed with you now. Shocking, I know. But that's how it is." His smile wavered. "I didn't realize how badly you were hurt before."

"They shot me with a poisoned dart," I whispered, staring up at him through half-lidded eyes.

He clasped me against his chest. His heartbeat thrummed in my ear. "It was almost enough to kill you. Almost. But..." He held up his clawless hand. It was so strange to see him with such an ordinary flesh coloration. He fluttered his fingers in front of my face. "Look who isn't diseased or cursed!"

"And you were a dragon," I murmured. "A raven dragon."

He nodded, his throat bobbing. Tears misted his eyes. "It was so easy. Like that's what I was made to be. I think...I wasn't a failure or a disappointment after all. That magic—it kept me in the eel and human forms and whatever I could do in between. But the raven dragon—I've never felt anything like it. I was so angry when I saw them attacking you, and—after the mate bond snapped into place and all of the king's magic fell away—the raven dragon form came to me even easier than the eel form. I flew. At least one of my parents was a raven dragon. And I was named for them. It wasn't a mistake or a mockery."

"Corvin." I smiled, savoring his name.

He grinned, nodding. He traced patterns on my cheek. "I didn't disappoint them because I could only become an eel. The King of the North Sea lied about everything."

"Maybe we'll find your family out there."

"Maybe. But I know I have family, here in my arms," he said softly. "Whatever happens—" He stopped then. His brow furrowed, then his eyes shuttered. "First, all jokes aside…I don't want to trap you in this." He took my hand in his, stroking it. "If you want to go your own way, I will let you. I'll even help you get to a town or a village."

I laughed, looking up at him. My heart was so full it was almost bursting. "You aren't getting rid of me that easily."

"Well then," he said, standing. He prodded Tagger away and helped me to my feet as well.

I swayed for half a breath before steadying myself on a birch. The warm golden sunlight surrounded us, birdsong flitting in the air.

With a smile, he knelt on one knee in front of me, still holding my hand. His hair was still fluffy and black and so soft, even if his black clothing was tattered and rent in too many places. "I've heard this is how humans proclaim their need for a mate."

My eyes widened. "Oh?" My stomach fluttered. "I mean, yes, this is how many propose marriage."

"And marriage is similar to mates, yes?" Corvin asked, still holding on to my hand.

I shrugged a little. "Are you asking me if I want to be with you officially, Corvin?" My face hurt from smiling so much. It was rather humorous to consider since I would have put a mate bond above any other.

He grinned, then steeled his face in a more somber expression. His eyes sparkled with lively mischief. "I want to spend the rest of my life with you, Mena. Do you want to spend yours with me?"

"I do," I said, tears brimming in my eyes. Part of me wanted to laugh at how serious he was being about this, and yet I loved it as well.

His eyebrow arched. "And what else do you want, Mena? I'll give you anything. I'll give you the world or I'll drown it. I'll do anything so long as it makes you happy."

"You're offering me the whole world?" I smiled down at him, heat burning through my core and up into my face. "Is that what you think I want?"

His gaze softened. He stood. His thumb pressed against my lower lip. "You're right." His fingers curled along my cheek then. "I see you. I love you. I want you. You are my light, my heart, and my home. And if anyone ever tries to take you from me, I'll tear them to pieces and give you their bones."

"And I will never abandon you, Corvin," I whispered. "I'll stay with you through dark passages and on bright paths." My lips trembled. "I love you with all I am."

He swept me close, his mouth claiming mine.

The rest of the world melted away with that kiss. His tongue pressed against the seam of my lips, urging them to part. I happily responded. It was nothing but us here. And the world spread out around us, full of joy and so much possibility. Dreams no longer felt pointless. It was as if it was all opening up once more in a realm of possibilities. Not what I had expected or planned for but beautiful in its own right.

When at last we broke the kiss, he kept his arms around me, and I left my hands in his hair. Tagger scampered around us, peeping and squeaking happily.

"We should probably see about a camp," I suggested, nuzzling him.

"Always so practical. At least you're accepting my compliments now," he murmured, smiling. "I suppose if you insist. It would be nice to have a place to stay." His hand lowered on my hips and squeezed. "Soon I'll give you the home you deserve. Someplace where you'll be safe and happy."

I hugged him once more, leaning up on my toes. "As long as I'm with you, I'm home."

He cradled me even closer. "And you will always be mine."

Thank you for joining me on this adventure, travelers. If you'd be so inclined as to leave a review, I'd greatly appreciate it.

And if you'd like the adventure to continue, hop over to: https://jmbutlerauthor.com/trapped-by-claws-bonuses/

And yes, if you are one of my dear readers who enjoys a little more steam, there will be a steamy scene included on this page as well as some extra bonuses and fun!

ABOUT THE AUTHOR

Jessica M. Butler is an adventurer, author, and attorney who never outgrew her love for telling stories and playing in imaginary worlds. She is the author of the epic fantasy romance series *Tue-Rah Chronicles* including *Identity Revealed*, *Enemy Known*, and *Princess Reviled*, *Wilderness Untamed*, *Shifter King* along with independent novellas *Locked*, *Cursed*, and *Alone*, set in the same world. She has also written numerous fantasy tales such as *Mermaid Bride*, *Little Scapegoat*, *Through the Paintings Dimly*, *Why Yes, Bluebeard, I'd Love To*, and more. For the most part, she writes speculative fiction with a heavy focus on multicultural high fantasy and suspenseful adventures and passionate romances. She lives with her husband and law partner, James Fry, in rural Indiana where they are quite happy with their five cats: Thor, Loptr, Fenrir, Hela, and Herne.

For more books or updates:
www.jmbutlerauthor.com

Read More from Jessica M. Butler

(jmbutlerauthor.com)

facebook.com/jmbutler1728
x.com/jessicabfry
instagram.com/jessicambutlerauthor

ALSO BY JESSICA M. BUTLER

Standalones

Of Serpents and Ruins

Bound By Blood

Through the Paintings Dimly

The Mermaid Bride

The Tue-Rah Chronicles

Identity Revealed

Enemy Known

Princess Reviled

Wilderness Untamed

Shifter King

Empire Undone

Tue-Rah Tales

Locked

Alone

Cursed

Standalones

Bound By Blood

Through the Paintings Dimly

The Mermaid Bride

Vellas

Fae Rose Bride

Made in the USA
Monee, IL
06 May 2025